IRONHEAD

by MEL ELLIS
IRONHEAD
SOFTLY ROARS THE LION
RUN, RAINY, RUN
SAD SONG OF THE COYOTE

IRONHEAD

by MEL ELLIS

HOLT, RINEHART AND WINSTON
New York   Chicago   San Francisco

For my grandchildren Christopher,
Dawn, Cinnamon and . . .

IRONHEAD

CHAPTER 1

The snake was halfway down a hole in an outcrop of limestone when I got a handhold on it. Then, there I stood. The snake couldn't go deeper, and I couldn't pull it out.

Maybe it wasn't the biggest rattlesnake in the world, and then again, maybe it was. It was nearly twice as long as I was tall and almost as thick around as my thigh.

Lucky for me it was a chilly morning. Big Swampy, which is in the heart of the vast Florida Everglades, hadn't come alive yet. If there had been a blazing sun, that big snake might have been quicker to coil and strike. And who knows, but to come suddenly and unexpectedly on a rattler of that size just might have been the end of me—Douglas Doucette, dead at seventeen. Not that I was frightened. Snake hunting was my business. But things happen.

The snake twisted and turned. I could feel my hands slipping, and every time I gave an inch, the snake took it and went deeper.

I hung on for what seemed like an hour, with the sun getting higher and hotter. Then the sweat began to run and my hands began to slip. No matter how hard I gripped, they slid down that narrowing tail. Then, all of a sudden, the snake writhed free and wriggled down the hole, and I stood with one rattle that had torn off its tail.

I put the rattle in my pocket and, breathing hard, dropped to my knees. After my breathing slowed, I crawled on my hands and knees across the sand into the shadow of a pine and, with my back against the tree, rested.

Well, there for sure went five hundred dollars down a hole. I'd seen the snake pass between two trees that were at least eight feet apart, so I knew it was the rattler that snake hunters dream about. Even while I'd been hanging to it, I'd seen myself walking into the Diamond Springs Reptile Institute at Hyacinth City and saying: "There's your eight-footer, Mr. Shen! There's the one you offer to pay five hundred dollars for, the one nobody—but nobody—in thirty years has ever found!"

You can't help dreaming like that if you're a snake hunter. You catch a hundred or five hundred little fellows from a foot to five feet long, and it gets to be like pulling night crawlers from the ground. And you scrounge out a living at the dollar a foot Don Shen pays, but you always look for that big one.

Getting to my feet to hike toward the shack, I told myself I'd be back. So long as there was an eight-footer on the loose, I'd be hunting for it, because right now I needed that money—more than anything else in the world.

By the time I hit a game trail back toward the shack, the dew had gone from the grass and birds were flashes of color in the hot sun. I didn't feel much like hunting now, but I checked out the likely places anyway, so it was late afternoon when I neared home.

At the edge of the clearing in which the shack stood I paused. Dad was on his log like he always was, just sitting like he was a part of the big piece of wood. Even from where I stood, I could see the deep lines on his face, and how his hair, once so soft and reddish brown, was dry and lifeless and turning gray. He was staring off into space, but not seeing anything. I'd seen him sit like that a hundred times, but it never got any easier.

Sometimes he didn't seem like my dad. He had been a big man, but now he seemed shriveled. His eyes went back into his head and had the same blank stare I'd seen on a skull we'd dug up one day while trying to scare an otter out of a mound on a palm hammock.

His hands, which he had once used to draw pictures in the air when he talked, just lay in his lap now, and the fingers curled back toward the wrists like a cripple's. And the bones of his shoulders stuck up like wing stubs under his blue shirt. It had happened to him when Mom died. No two people had been closer.

It was a while yet to suppertime and, after what had happened, I couldn't see myself just sitting around in front of the shack looking at the hollow emptiness of Dad's eyes and talking to him, but never getting any answers. So I backed quietly away before he knew I was there and walked to a special place of mine where I could sit awhile and think.

Evening was easing in when I came down the long arrowing lane of pines and broke out of the trees to my special place on a stump. With the sun slanting, the sea of saw grass on all sides was turning from a dusty yellow to a shiny gold. And there, a short distance away, Cypress Pond, ringed with trees, blazed green and cool.

I sat on the stump often to think, though I knew nothing would come of it. But it sort of soothed me, and then there was an old gator lived in the pond, and he was company of a kind.

Long ago, before Mom had died, Dad had named the gator Ironhead, like he sometimes used to call me. He, Old Ironhead, was always there. You could depend on him, so when I'd get on the stump I'd grunt like an old bull alligator, and he'd grunt right back at me.

When we'd lived in town I was lucky if I got out to Cypress Pond once a week. Evenset, where we'd lived, wasn't very big—just a sprawl of houses at a crossroads with shacks dripping over into Big Swampy, and it had taken me two hours to walk all the way to the pond.

I had always thought I'd live my life in Evenset, but after Mom died and when Gaylord Wiggens came to get the rent, Dad had said we were moving. That's when we came out to the shack Dad had built for weekends and vacations.

4

At the time I had been glad, because out in Big Swampy, away from the things that reminded him of Mom, I thought Dad might get better. But he got worse instead, much worse.

I didn't grunt to Ironhead this night, what with losing the big snake and thinking about how things were, I didn't have the heart for it. So, when the sun started to set, I got up and took the path through the Piny Woods back to the shack.

That night it rained. It came down on the roof like the heavens were falling in. The Glades get rains like that and then water comes down in solid sheets. But it stopped before morning, and everything was so sparkling fresh I left early to hunt because we were just about out of everything, and a man has got to eat.

By the time I got to the high ground where a ramshackle litter of old logs had all but disappeared under vines, the sun had gotten high enough to get through to the sand and start warming the world.

Almost at once I spotted a snake. It was near the clutter of logs in a patch of dry grass. It was darting its tongue in and out to test the air, so I knew I had to get between it and the old buildings fast, or it would slither under and into a den.

I braced myself for a flying start and then leaped between the snake and the logs. The snake slithered around and then coiled into striking position and, lifting its head, sampled the air again.

I was just out of striking range, and it didn't have to

5

be told I was there. It could taste me on the air just as I had tasted butter on my morning grits.

This was pure plain luck to come across a snake right away. Sometimes I went for days without even seeing a two-footer, and this was a good one—five feet, anyway.

Five dollars, I thought. It would be enough to get all the rice and grits, flour and salt we needed, and there'd be money for meat and butter and even some canned peaches.

I took a step toward the snake and its rattles whirred like loose seeds rustling around in a dry gourd. Just out of range, I put a foot forward for it to strike, and it did, getting hold of the edge of my boot bottom. In the same instant I broke contact, side-stepped, and quickly brought the forked stick down in back of its head and pinned it to the sand.

Its tail began threshing, and to keep it from hurting itself, I bent quickly and, getting a firm grip with thumb and forefinger right in back of the head, lifted it and in the same lifting motion popped out the sack tied to my side and slid the snake in.

It wriggled for a while in the sack, and then when it quieted, I started back down the trail.

I could still make the noon bus, and then come back on the three o'clock and be at the shack with my groceries before sundown.

Before I got to the highway it turned hot, and when I broke out of the scrub the concrete was swimming in heat waves. I looked at the sun and figured I was just about on time, and no sooner had I sat in the shade of a scrub oak when I heard the bus humming in the distance, and then I saw the smoke of the exhaust trailing it like a blue flag.

I got up and walked out onto the shoulder of the road and didn't even have to raise my arm, because the driver saw me and started braking so that the tires squealed and the bus grunted, and then it stopped and the door swung open.

"See you got another," the driver said, as I swung up and handed him the fifty-cent piece I'd been saving for the trip.

CHAPTER 2

The bus was nearly full, and I had to take a seat along the aisle, next to a woman in a blue bonnet. Mostly there were Crackers on their way to Hyacinth City to shop—mothers with bunches of bashful kids, all barefoot and in overalls and nothing else.

I don't know why people look down on them and call them "Crackers," but I once heard Don Shen say it was because there was no nut too tough for them to crack. They lived in the back country, and Don had said they were as bashful as they were brave, and born and bred right up out of the black earth and not beholding to anybody because of it.

But there were some tourists in the bus too, and they were headed for Diamond Springs: men in shirts on fire with flowers and hats of such shiny straw they glinted like gold, and women with bare shoulders lifting like white hills out of tight, bright dresses.

The tourists gawked at the Crackers, but the Crackers didn't gawk back. They looked straight ahead, brown people compared to the tourists, all with that blank look which means they know they are being gawked at.

The tourists were eying them like they were orphaned fawns. Maybe they looked poor, but they didn't need any sympathy, and it made me so mad I felt like I wanted to spit on the floor in front of them.

A couple of women were trying to win over two skinny, brown kids, but the kids wouldn't take their eyes off the floor while the women hunted through their purses for pennies. The women cawed back and forth until a tanned man in a tan business suit said: "Don't be so cheap! Give them dimes."

The women stopped cawing and gave the man an uppity look, but he only laughed, and inside of the minute they were back at it again, and then one found a penny and held it out and the boy snatched it up like it was a hundred dollars, but he didn't look up, and when the woman said, "Well, that's gratitude for you," the mother drew the boy onto her lap and took the penny from him and handed it back to the woman. Then the man in the business suit laughed again and the women quit cawing.

I leaned against the seat rest then, and the hum of the tires and the steady roar of the engine made me sleepy, so I braced for a nap and fell asleep thinking about that big snake and how maybe by tomorrow, he'd be brave enough to come out from his den, and then I'd be waiting for him with an extra-strong forked

9

stick and one sack stuffed inside another to give it strength.

Then I had one of my favorite dreams: I was back in the white house in Evenset, out on the back stoop with a thick slice of homemade bread dripping with real cream and heaped with brown sugar, and my mother was sitting under the trestle where the bougainvillaea climbed, and she was talking to my dad, who had the hood of the big truck up and was bent over inside working on the motor.

My mother's voice was always sweet and clear and distinct as the sound of bells, but my dad's voice was always a mumble coming from deep inside the huge hood of the truck, and I could never make out what it was he said. His voice always came to me in the dream like the distant rumble of thunder; it disturbed me that I couldn't understand him, and I'd stop chewing on the bread and lean forward to try and make out the words.

And my mother would always be saying the same thing. She'd be telling my dad that he shouldn't work on Sunday and to come sit beside her in the shade and have a cool glass of lemonade.

"You work too hard, Duke," she'd say. "You shouldn't, you know. We should take more time just for ourselves, because who knows?"

Then she'd sigh, and Dad would say something from down under the hood, and I knew without hearing the words that he would be saying: "Nobody ever got anywhere without working. If you think I want to be poor as a Cracker the rest of my life...."

There was this one thing about him, he wouldn't settle for being "poor as a Cracker," and it was the one thing that didn't fit, because all his friends were Crackers and he truly liked them.

But I'd feel good sitting there watching my dad work and seeing the smile on my mother's pretty red mouth, and the cream would drip to my chin and I'd catch it with a finger and then lick the finger, and. . . .

A scream ended my dream and just about jarred me through the roof of the bus. But, even before I turned, I knew it had come from one of the fat tourist women, because there wasn't anybody else aboard with that much lung power.

It wasn't only one scream, but one right after another. Couple of times I've heard panthers away back in a swamp, and that is what they sounded like. Only a panther would scream once and then take a breather, but this woman kept right on screaming and, when I looked back, I saw the other one had fainted.

The bus driver swung in his seat and almost spun the bus right off the road. He recovered quickly enough, and then he eased the big tires off onto the sandy shoulder and I could feel the bus tilt a little as the wheels went lower. But I still didn't know what the woman was screaming about unless a gator flea had somehow gotten on the bus and had its pincers into her. But even a gator flea, which is hardly bigger than a little finger, was too small a critter for all that screaming, and when I heard a Cracker whisper:

"Snake!"

I ducked my head down quickly to look under the seat, and the sack lay so flat that there couldn't be anything in it, and the twine I had tied it with was lying in a loop just the way it had slipped off.

The word went around fast. Nobody said it aloud. It went around the bus like a hiss: "Snake! Snake! Snake!" And I got to my knees to look along the floor, but all at once there were so many feet and legs I couldn't see a thing.

The tourists were up and scrambling around, but the Crackers sat tight waiting, except the mothers pulled the children in a little closer, and I couldn't help noticing that one wrinkled old guy with a nose which hooked almost down to his chin cackled, and if the corners of his toothless mouth hadn't been turned up, nobody would have guessed it was a laugh.

When the bus finally stopped and the doors flew open, the tourists began piling out of there like turtles off a log when a hawk swoops over. But the Crackers only lifted their children to their laps and sat like statues.

The bus driver left the wheel and stood behind his seat shouting for everybody to sit still, but the tourists kept piling over one another until I thought that any who didn't get bitten would surely be trampled to death.

The woman who had done all the screaming finally shut up long enough to pull herself out into the aisle, and then she started toward the door only to come hip to hip with the man in the tan business suit. There they stuck between the arm rests of the aisle seats and the man looked sick and the woman started screaming again.

I'd have laughed if it hadn't been serious and if it hadn't been *my* snake. She was waving her arms like she was trying to swim on air, and the man was turning white as a piece of paper under his tan as she squeezed him tighter and tighter.

Maybe it was because I started feeling sorry for the poor man, but anyway I planted both hands right in the middle of the fat woman's back and, bracing on the seat, I popped her forward and she went down the aisle like the cork out of a bottle of home brew.

She nearly knocked the bus driver over when she went by, and then out on the shoulder she staggered through the shallow ditch and went into a flowery heap of dress under a live oak.

By that time the other fat woman had come around, but nothing moved on her except her mouth, which was trembling, and the tears that rolled down her cheeks. She was frozen there, and I knew that snake wouldn't hit her if she stayed frozen.

I don't know how long it took, because everything was pretty wild for a while, but finally all the tourists were out on the side of the road and only the Crackers and the woman who couldn't move were left.

"Okay, Doug," the bus driver said, and he said it cool and calm and quiet. "Find the snake."

He didn't look mad, but he didn't look happy. I got to my hands and knees, got hold of the sack, and moved up the aisle toward the rear of the bus, looking carefully under each seat as I went by.

I looked especially long and carefully when I saw the fat lady's legs, but there was no snake there. Inside the bus it was so quiet I could hear the fat lady's wrist watch ticking, and I swear I could hear her heart beating.

Outside, the tourists, brave now, were shouting to the bus driver to get his passengers off and to safety. But some were laughing like it had been nothing but a fire drill, only the laughing had a cracked edge to it.

None of the Crackers moved while I looked for the snake. They knew it was down there somewhere, but they also knew that if they sat perfectly quiet there was a good chance that snake would pass them right on by without so much as flicking its tongue.

I found the rattler under the last seat, about a foot from a man's leg. The snake was trying to get under the rubber floor covering. I came up behind it as slowly as a bobcat coming up on a quail. I put one hand down and then one knee, and then the other hand and the other knee. Then I lowered myself like a bobcat crouching to make its leap. Right down to my elbows I went, so my head and shoulders fit under the seat. Then when my right hand was about a foot from that snake, I put all my weight on the left elbow, so I could really move the free hand.

I breathed slowly and deeply and held it. Then I flicked out my arm and like that I had the snake just below the head. I couldn't get it into the sack under the seat, so I had to stand, and when the big woman saw me with five feet of snake hanging from my right hand, she fainted again. Then I popped it into the sack and walked toward the front of the bus.

"Doug, you gave me a scare. Whatever happened?" the driver asked.

I didn't know for sure myself, but I thought maybe it was the heat because of so many people on the bus. It had been sweltering, so I said: "It must have gotten too hot, and that snake just started working around in that sack until it slipped the string. Too much heat or too much cold makes them move and they're awful powerful when they start writhing."

"Well, you'll have to walk from here," he said, "because those yahoos will never get back on the bus so long as the snake is aboard."

I nodded and said it would be all right, and that I was sorry it had happened.

"It's just one of those things," the driver said. "Just lucky nobody got bitten or died of a heart attack." He slipped the fifty-cent piece into my hand.

I thanked him, and when I swung down to the road the tourists parted to let me through like I was the snake. I walked back to the scrub edge and sank down on the ground.

"It's all right now," the driver was calling out. "He has the snake. You can all come back aboard and we'll get on to Diamond Springs."

They started clambering aboard then, and all at once they were brave again and telling each other how if they had known just where it was they'd have stomped the life out of it—all except one couple, and they were giving the bus driver a hard time, and telling him how they were going to report him, and that I *didn't* like.

I was afraid the couple just might report the driver, and then he might be in trouble. During the past month we'd gotten to be friends, even though we only exchanged a few words each time he picked me up.

The tourists were squirming back into their seats and looking under them to make sure another snake wasn't crawling about, and still the Crackers hadn't said a word, nor did they look at the tourists, but sat looking straight ahead just as though nothing had happened, except when the bus started one woman Cracker sitting on the ditch side turned her head to me and smiled and lifted her hand as much as to say:

"Good luck."

It was the woman I had been seated next to, but I didn't wave back, because I couldn't be sure she had waved to me, but I wanted to think she had, because it took away the feeling of being all alone.

I waited almost an hour before I got a lift, and I told the driver right out that I had a snake in the bag so there'd be no trouble, and he just laughed and said to put it on the back seat, "because I gotta be in Diamond Springs but right now!"

He was a youngish fellow with round, red cheeks and a mouth that always looked like it was laughing about some private little joke of its own. He said he was with a drug distributing company from upstate, and that he made Diamond Springs once or twice a week to pick up venom for the laboratories.

Then I told him the snake was for Mr. Shen, and he said that he knew it was.

I told him about the snake getting loose in the bus, and about how the tourists had almost trampled one another getting off. I told him about the fat lady screaming and how I thought she'd squash the skinny man to death and how I'd pushed her on down the aisle, and he began laughing like he'd never stop.

"I'd give a week's salary," he said, "to have seen that. Tourists mostly give me a pain. They've never been off a sidewalk, and they couldn't live one night if you turned them loose in the Glades, but they look down their noses at the Crackers and act like they came straight to Florida as a gift from God. Give me the Crackers anytime. They *really* know what life is all about."

I said maybe he was right, and then I said I supposed I was a Cracker because Dad and I sure were poor enough.

"What do you think I am?" he asked. "Most of my life I lived right on the edge of not eating. I was born and raised and ran away from a shack not more than thirty miles from here."

"But you aren't Cracker any more," I said.

"That's what you think. Once a Cracker, always a Cracker."

"But you've got money. You're driving a big car. You've got good clothes and a good job, and you've...."

He put his right hand up to stop me. "Listen, son," he said, "being a Cracker has nothing to do with any dictionary definition about being a poor white."

"But most of us are poor," I pointed out.

"Well, maybe a little short on cash," he said, "but when it comes to plain gumption and the ability to solve our own problems, we're richer than most. We don't go asking for anything. They can keep their charity. A Cracker doesn't need it."

I had to agree that it was a wonderful way to look at it, but I also thought that I'd trade some of that gumption for good hard cash to put Dad in the hospital. That was the trouble with being poor. Get sick and you had it. You were helpless.

That's the only reason I was afraid they'd put Dad in The Institution—because we didn't have any money to put him anywhere else.

I knew about The Institution. They'd sent Dummy Bergen there, and everybody in Evenset said it was nothing but a nut house, and that Dummy was a nut.

Poor Dummy. He'd never hurt anybody. Like Dad he'd just sort of quit living.

The man at the wheel was quiet for the moment and I remembered how Doc Bellamy—that's Doctor Benjamin Bellamy—had laid it on the line for me.

"Douglas, you're about a man now, so I'm going to talk to you like a man," he'd said. "You know Duke is sick, don't you?" Duke is Dad's name. Duke Doucette.

I just nodded and he went on. "Doug, your dad needs help."

He hadn't fooled me, not after what had happened to Dummy Bergen. But he did leave me some hope. One thing he said was that if I could get up enough money, there was a good chance his illness might be cured at a psychiatric hospital he knew about. And second, he said that in cases like Dad's, sometimes a sudden shock seemed to bring them out of their dream world.

"If they get God-awful scared for someone they love, it sometimes jars them back to life," was the way Doc had put it.

I left off thinking about Dad because the man at the wheel was talking again: "I know millionaire Crackers and I know good doctors and good lawyers who wouldn't admit to being anything else. Being a Cracker doesn't mean any more than making the best of what you got whether it's a little or a lot."

He was quiet for a while, like he'd just delivered a sermon and I was to think on it. He sure gave me a good feeling, about myself and about him. I felt comfortable with him right off, and for me that is unusual, because usually I don't take to people.

Then he told me his name was Ranney Bowles, and that he usually made the trip to Diamond Springs on Thursday—in case I was looking for a ride.

"But I get down on other days too, especially if Don calls to say he's got a lot of venom to get rid of."

I thanked him for the offer of other rides and said I just might be watching along the road come Thursday, because it wasn't likely the bus driver would be allowed to let me ride again with a snake, and it was surely too far to walk.

"It would be a pleasure, and I'd take you back except that usually I have to head downstate a ways," Mr. Bowles said, and then we were turning into the Diamond Springs Reptile Institute driveway and under the big archway and up to the main building where the offices were.

I reached around and got my snake and thanked Mr. Bowles for the ride, and he held out his hand and we shook, and then he went in and I walked around back to the small building where the snakes were received.

Mr. Shen wasn't there, but then he was often away. He did a big business, sometimes buying five thousand snakes a year. He had gators too, lots of them. But most of the gators he raised right on his own place. I'd seen him wrestle a ten-footer. He did it as slick as anything. Sometimes he wrestled gators for the tourists, but mostly now he had some Seminole Indian boys come in and he trained them to do it for him.

A man I knew as Mike was behind the desk, and when I came in he got up.

"Big one?" Mike asked.

"Fair," I said.

He took the bag from me, and walking to an empty concrete pit with high wire cemented above it, he gently slid the snake out onto the cool floor. The rattler lay still for a few seconds, and then it began to feel the air with its tongue to see where it was. Finally it stretched and began to crawl.

"A good five feet. A dandy! Healthy too," Mike said, and he walked over to the desk and made out a slip that would tell the office help in the main building that I was to be paid for a six-foot instead of a five-foot rattler, and there was a dollar bonus.

I thanked him when he handed me the slip, and I

wanted to tell him about the excitement on the bus to see if he would think it was funny, but decided against it when he bent over some papers and began to write.

Back out in the sun again, I started walking toward the main building when I felt eyes on me and heard whispering. I turned, and there, sure enough, were the tourists who had been on the bus, and they had recognized me. They were walking along the gravel path looking at Mr. Shen's exhibits, but now they seemed more interested in me than the snakes or the gators.

I put my head down and looked at the stones underfoot, hurrying a little to get away because I didn't feel so good now about what I had been thinking and saying about them. Just before I got to the main building I felt a hand on my arm, and I stopped and turned.

It was one of the tourists, and I sort of remembered he had been sitting just across from me.

"I want to apologize for my friends and myself," the man said.

"No call for it," I said, looking down again.

"You must understand," the man continued, "that these people just don't know and understand snakes. Even a little grass snake is enough to scare them right out of their skins."

I looked up at the man then. "It doesn't matter," I said.

"But it does matter, if only because you are a boy," the man went on. "But they are good people and they are also brave in their own way. They'll stare a truck driver to a dead stop in traffic, which would probably scare you half to death."

I looked up then and he seemed embarrassed about trying to explain it to me, and now I felt even worse, so I said there was no call for his feeling bad, because I knew just how it was. I said: "I know what you mean. I've seen girls run from frogs and then swim a fast river like it was nothing at all."

The man smiled and patted my arm, and then he went back to where the tourists were, and I thought how it was everybody wanted to look their best in someone else's eyes, and maybe that was good.

When I gave the slip to the girl at the desk I saw Mr. Shen over in a corner talking to Ranney Bowles, and when he saw me he waved and I waved back.

I couldn't help thinking how quick Mr. Shen was. It's no wonder he could handle snakes and gators. He was even quick in the way he waved and the way his eyes moved. Even his fingers were fast, and the only thing about him that wasn't fast were words, and they came slow.

All along I'd been thinking about how much fun it would be to tell Mr. Shen about the excitement on the bus, but now it didn't seem so funny, so when the girl gave me a five-dollar bill and a one, I just turned and left because I had to hurry now to get groceries so I could make the late bus, and even then I'd have to walk the last hour in the dark, and I didn't like leaving Dad sitting out there after the sun had gone down.

So I trotted most of the way to the store, and passed up the supermarket to go into the little store which was like the one Winnie Dean ran in Evenset.

CHAPTER 3

❧ The sun was just setting when I swung off the bus and felt sand underfoot. I lit right out and was a good piece back in the scrub before the sound of the bus died away. But even though I walked fast, it was full dark before I was halfway home, and I had to slow down to keep the wait-a-bit bushes from tearing at me.

The rain from the night before had brought out thick clouds of mosquitoes. I didn't mind their bite, because when I was little Dad had taken me into Big Swampy and we had sat most of one night just letting the mosquitoes eat on us.

It had been a night. It was pure, plain, crazy torture, and every time I'd smack at the mosquitoes, Dad would say: "Let them bite you."

But even if I'd had six hands I couldn't have kept

them off. They came in so thick to the light of a tiny fire we had that sometimes I couldn't see my arm for wriggling, winging, crawling mosquitoes.

The whine coming from the clouds of them hovering over us was like that of a buzz saw eating steadily and surely through a pine log without a letup. Then after a while it wasn't the noise of a buzz saw, but something that had gotten inside my head.

I had been a mess the next morning. There wasn't a square inch on me that wasn't red and swollen, and I could hardly see because my eyelids were so puffed.

Mother had cried and given Dad one scolding right after another.

"It's criminal, Duke. It is positively criminal. To take a youngster like that and subject him to such torture. Do you realize he could die from the infection?"

Then Dad showed his arm to Mother and said: "Look. Do you see any bites on me? You want to know why? Because thanks to my dad, when I was a boy, he did the same thing to me. You want him to fight mosquitoes the rest of his life or get it over with in one night?"

And to tell the truth, the swelling went down after a dozen baths in baking-soda water, and after that mosquitoes never bothered me any more. I might feel a prick when they'd sting me, but I was even used to that. And no matter how many times I got stung, it never so much as raised a pimple, nor did I ever have an itch worth scratching.

So I was always glad Dad had taken me into the

swamp and given me the mosquito treatment, because tonight I could walk right through them; flies would have bothered me more.

By the time I was within calling distance of the shack, a near-full moon lifted over the edge of the far trees and turned everything silver. I was anxious now. I always worried when I was away after dark, because I never could be sure what Dad would do.

Coming down the trail I strained forward to see if he was sitting on the log. He wasn't there. Neither was there a light in the shack, so I started trotting and when I got a stone's throw from the door I called out: "Dad! Dad? You there?"

But even though I didn't expect an answer, I suddenly felt afraid, so I turned on the speed and burst through the open door of the shack, and then I saw him silhouetted against a moonlighted window.

"You gave me a scare, Dad," I said. "The least you could do would be to answer me so I'd know you are okay. And don't tell me you've lost your voice, because I know darn well you haven't. Sometimes I think you just want to scare me. Darn it, Dad, don't you think of anybody except yourself?"

I had never talked to him like that before, but my fright had turned to anger, and it didn't seem right that he should put me through something like that—anyway, not after the kind of day I'd had.

So I swung my rattlesnake bag full of groceries into a corner and lighted a kerosene lamp, and when its yellow light spread into the corners and I could see Dad's face, I was sorry I had been angry with him and went over and took him by the arm and led him to a chair by the table.

Then I noticed that he had only one shoe on. It wasn't surprising. He'd lost so much weight, even his shoes were loose on his feet and he slopped around in them. But I asked anyway: "Where's your shoe, Dad? Did you lose it?" And I watched his face and thought I saw a flicker of understanding and something which looked almost like fear.

"What's the matter, Dad?" I asked and sat across the table from him to see better. But his face had gone blank again, so I went about slicing some of the ham I'd bought, and after a fire was going I slid the skillet over the heat.

When the tin plates had been wiped and put away and I'd gotten Dad into his bunk, I looked around the shack for the shoe, but it wasn't there.

Then I went outside to the log where he'd been sitting, and though the moonlight made everything bright and white as day, I couldn't see a shoe anywhere.

That was strange, because Dad hardly ever moved from the log. After I was sure the shoe wasn't near the log, I searched along the path to the outhouse, which stood among some palmettos a short way back of the shack. But it wasn't along the path either.

The shoe didn't matter. It was only a cut-down, old snake boot, but the fact that he'd been moving around somewhere that I didn't know about did matter.

It must be that once I left he would get up from the log and do some walking. It could be a good sign, and then again, maybe it wasn't. I didn't like him to be roaming around. He might get lost or even blunder into a snake or a boar. But then again, if he was moving, maybe he was starting to take notice of things.

Well, I wasn't going to worry about it tonight. I was beat, so I slipped out of my clothes and crawled under the blanket.

The hooty owls were enjoying the night; even they needed some light to see by, and on a moonlighted night such as this they really could get in some good hunting and surely go to bed in the morning full of food. And they were celebrating the fact and kept calling back and forth to one another just as though they were saying:

"Well, how about this! Did you ever see such a night! In all my born days I haven't opened my eyes to such a bright moon! Just look!"

But then I fell asleep, and I guess I must have slept like a dead man, because when I awakened the moon was gone from the east and shining through the west window, and both my arms were asleep and I could hardly move them to get the blood running so they'd tingle alive.

I looked over at Dad, and the moon was in his face and he wasn't sleeping, but just staring at the ceiling. I knew he didn't sleep much, but lay there just looking, because on other moonlighted nights I'd see his eyes wide open and staring.

I'd had a terrible dream too. It seemed lately I dreamed every night. This time I was on the bus again, and I kept shoving the big lady and every time she popped forward she would turn around, and then she would be Dad and he'd give me a hurt look.

I fell asleep and started to dream the dream again, but then it was morning and I was glad to be done with that night, glad to start a new day.

I thought maybe this day I'd check on the big snake and keep an eye open for a young pig. I'd heard some squealing back off in a patch of scrub about a week ago, but when I'd gone in the pigs had left. From the tracks it looked like an old sow with a litter that should be just about weaned. The young would be easy to catch, and a small pig would feed us for a few days, and it always helped keep the grocery bill down.

Before going I looked around again for the shoe, but couldn't find it, and after I had Dad fed and he went out to the log with only one shoe on, I thought maybe I ought to take the shoe away from him because it looked funny, but then decided that it didn't make any difference if he was wearing only one shoe, because who was going to see him, and so long as it didn't bother him, why should it bother me?

I took three gunny sacks and on the way down the trail took out my knife to cut a really stout stick with a wide fork, and then I headed to where I'd had hold of the big snake.

On the way I went through the place I called The Church, and I stopped in the center of the live oaks for a few minutes just to get the feel of being separated from the glaring world, and while I was standing there, I made a promise to myself that I'd take the day off tomorrow and go fishing at Mirror River.

Sitting in The Church, with the moss draped down all around to keep out the heat and the sun, was almost as good as lying back on the sandy banks of the river and watching a pine sliver bobber for signs of bream biting. I always felt a little guilty when I spent a day fishing, but I'd tell myself that it was good for both of us to get fish to eat once in awhile, and that helped some.

While resting in back of the hanging moss curtains, I got to thinking about Dad's shoe again. He sure must have wandered off somewhere, otherwise I'd have found that shoe around the shack.

Well, I'd find out sometime, and meanwhile there was the big snake, and thinking about it started me off again, and I pushed aside a shawl of moss and went from the cool shade into the hot sun.

As I walked I wondered why I hadn't mentioned the big snake to the drug salesman or told Mr. Shen about it, and then I guessed that I didn't because I could hardly believe it myself, and if I was having a hard time believing it, how could I make them believe it?

The offer of five hundred dollars had been standing for thirty years, and no one had ever brought in an eight-footer to collect it. Mr. Shen offered fifty dollars for seven-footers, and only three times in the thirty years did snake hunters collect the big money.

It was good that I hadn't said anything. If word ever got around that there was an eight-foot rattler in Big Swampy, there wouldn't be room for the men who would come hunting it. Word might even get back to Doc Bellamy that I'd seen a record breaking five-hundred-dollar snake and, knowing Doc Bellamy, he'd come looking, but not for the snake.

To get to the limestone outcrop where I'd had hold of the snake, I had to go near the pig hunter's old corrals, so I detoured a little to look in on them. But I didn't see any signs of a snake or any fresh trails in the sand.

I hurried a little after that, because now the sun was high and hot enough to bring any snake out into the open. When I got to the place where the snake had gone underground, I found my heel marks. They were so deep where I'd braced, even the rain hadn't washed them away.

I stood real still for a long time looking everything over, but there was no sign of the snake. Then I knelt in front of the hole and put my nose to it to smell. Rattlers give off a sort of damp, musty smell. But there was no fresh snake smell in the hole, which didn't surprise me, because that snake could have moved.

Actually, he could have gone a great distance underground, because I had once heard Dad say that the whole peninsula of Florida was so honeycombed underneath he wouldn't be surprised to see it all crumble some day and sink quietly into the sea. He had been half kidding and half not kidding. Because there's no doubt that there are thousands and thousands of passageways and underground rivers in Florida, especially in the Glades and Big Swampy.

If there wasn't, how could a dried up sinkhole on getting a fresh catch of rain water all of a sudden be filled with fish? Fish can't fly, that's for sure, and I haven't seen any walking around on shore, so they've got to come to the sinkholes through underground rivers.

Well, if that snake had traveled underground, he had to come up somewhere, and it wasn't likely he'd travel far before doing so. In that case, I'd have to hunt him out and there was no sense in doing it any way except thoroughly.

So I took out my knife, went over to a palmetto and hacked off a frond, and I threw it down to mark the spot where the snake hole was. Then I walked slowly in circles and kept widening the circles so I'd cover every bit of ground in the area.

Sometimes the path would take me through heavy scrub, and other times I'd be right out in the open where the sun could start the sweat popping right through my shirt. I didn't hurry, and I didn't make any more noise than I had to. If that snake was around, I was going to get him, and even if he was dead somewhere underground, I knew I'd keep on hunting for a long, long time, always hoping I'd some day be able to walk into Diamond Springs and say:

"Just look at this, Mr. Shen!"

By the time the sun was starting down the sky, I'd gotten a good hundred yards from the snake hole, so I lay down under a scrub oak to rest awhile.

31

It was so hot I didn't even see any buzzards, and except for one hawk so high it looked like a tiny fly, the sky was a whitish blue without a blur in it.

Today I wished I'd brought a little water. I was thirsty, but as much from the excitement of hoping to suddenly see the snake as from the heat. But I'd taught myself to go without water or food, and I felt better on two meals a day than when I also stuffed myself at noon.

Lying there, I closed my eyes for a little while and I could hear flies buzzing. In a little while I opened my eyes, and the short rest made me feel better all over, so I got up and started circling again, though I didn't have much hope.

Once I stopped by a small sinkhole and was tempted to drink some pond water, but decided against it. I drank some once without boiling it, and it hadn't done anything to me. And I had known hog hunters who always drank it. But one thing my mother insisted on when Dad and I would strike off into Big Swampy to hunt or fish was that we drink no pond water without boiling it first. The thought of all the crawling things in it went against her, so laughing a little, Dad made the promise and even if he laughed about it, he kept it.

After I'd circled so far away from the hole where the rattler had gone underground that I figured it would take me a half hour to walk back, I gave up on the big snake for that day.

The sun was getting down around four o'clock, and I started back so I'd have the evening for doing nothing except maybe visit Piny Woods to watch the sun go down, and maybe after dark grunting Old Ironhead close enough to get his red eyes into the jacklight.

I took a different route back, hoping to come across the litter of pigs I knew was somewhere in the scrub. Ever since the days of free range when pigs were allowed to run willy-nilly across the countryside, some had drifted into Big Swampy and turned wild. A shoat made good eating, if you could catch one.

Of course, I kept my eyes open for snakes. But watching for snakes took no effort. It was second nature with me. I used to think that if some day I ever lived in a city, I'd probably go down the sidewalk or along the road quiet and careful like I was expecting a snake to slide out from behind a fireplug or a parking meter.

When I hit the home path I put my hand in front of my eyes. The sun was still four fingers high. I hurried a little now, having been over this territory so many times I didn't think it likely there'd be any pigs around, or any snakes, for that matter.

When I came in sight of the shack, I could see Dad's bowed shoulders and his head sunk down in between them, and I automatically breathed a sigh of relief that he was where he ought to be and that nothing had happened while I was away.

Now I made a little noise like I always did when approaching the shack, so as not to startle him, and when I came into the clearing I said: "Hi, Dad. Have a good day?"

And he turned his head just that little bit so he could see me out the corner of an eye, and lifted the fingers of his right hand a few inches to signify that he'd heard me.

Right away I noticed that his other shoe was missing. I walked up to him and said: "Dad, now you've lost the other shoe. Where have you been that you could lose both shoes?"

But, of course, he didn't answer, so I dropped to my knees and examined his feet. There was mud on both of them and there was mud on his pants. So it was a cinch he'd gotten into a damp bottom somewhere. But there were dried up sinkholes all over the place, and there was enough mud in most to suck off a shoe and dirty his feet.

I put my stick and sacks beside the shack and started looking once again for his shoes. I walked the clearing through several times, examined the nearest sinkholes, went back and forth along the outhouse trail, and even looked down the one-holer to see if he had thrown them away. But there were no shoes.

I didn't like it, but it made me laugh, mostly at myself, and when I started supper I said: "Well, Dad, what's the mystery of the missing shoes? You going to tell me, or you going to make me spend the rest of my life wandering through Big Swampy looking for shoes when I should be hunting snakes?"

I talked a lot when I was around Dad, even though he didn't answer me. It seemed that I had to talk, that I had to hear my voice or else all this—the whole terrible predicament—would get so spooky and unreal I'd start losing my bearings just like Dad.

We ate leftover ham and some twist bread I made right on top of the stove with flour, salt, and water.

Then after the tin plates were washed and Dad was back out on the log with a cup of coffee, I started for the Piny Woods to sit for a spell and let the night coolness come down on me and sink into my bones so I'd be glad to come back to the shack and crawl under a blanket.

The heat was still like a wall to walk through when I made my way down the trail, but no sooner did the sun disappear below the far trees then the night cool came in, and I breathed as deep as I could to get the freshness of it clear through me.

Then I just sat and looked and there was a hawk doing some late hunting and an owl came out to do some early hunting. And maybe I'd just have sat there until it got black dark and then waited for the moon, except that something wasn't quite right out front and I knew it.

Being alone a lot in Big Swampy, I got so I could almost feel a change in the land around. Especially did I notice changes in areas where I most moved. I suppose it is something like the woman who comes to her kitchen and wonders who hung the dish towel in back of the door when it should be by the sink. There was something different about the land out front, so I stood to look.

Moving my eyes slowly across the clearing, I spotted it. Something big had been moving along the edge of Cypress Pond because I could see black marks where it had kicked up the mud. So I went down thinking to come on deer or pig tracks, maybe a big boar, and then I almost keeled over when I saw that they were man tracks.

Who in the whole, wide world. . . . Then it hit me. Dad! So I followed the tracks and, sure enough, first I found one shoe stuck in the muck, and then where another set of tracks came down I found the other.

He had come all the way to the water and then started in, but something had made him change his mind, because a few feet from where the tracks disappeared into the pond they came back out again.

But what? Why? And with Ironhead lying out there just waiting for a man to fall on his face. Now I really did have a problem.

CHAPTER 4

✺ I didn't sleep much that night. Of all places, Cypress Pond! I lay there with the blanket turned down a little, watching the moonlight creep across the floor, and I had to come to the conclusion that Dad just wasn't aimlessly wandering about, but that there was something down at Cypress Pond that he *wanted* or something that made him *want* to go there. But what?

Cypress Pond. For Dad it was a dangerous place. I couldn't let him wander around down there. But how could I keep on with my snake hunting and watch him at the same time?

If he didn't drown, I knew for sure that sooner or later Ironhead would swim over and that would be the end of that.

Old Ironhead might be frightened when caught high and dry, and if I came to the pond when he was

37

up on a mud bank sunning, he'd move like legged lightning to get back into the water. But in the pond I doubted that he was afraid of anything.

I had once seen an alligator come up on a swimming pig over in Mirror River, and to this day I could hear the pig's squeals as it went down. The gator, a ten-footer like Ironhead, had come up and gotten a leg hold, and then with a sweep of its tail it rolled, and the pig just turned over and went down like it'd been sucked under in a whirlpool of muddy water.

But maybe Dad wouldn't go back to Cypress Pond. Maybe he'd had enough of getting stuck in the muck and losing his shoes. Only I couldn't take a chance, and I'd have to watch him.

We had some groceries and two dollars left from the snake money, so perhaps I could slow down and devise some way of taking Dad with me and then plunking him on a cabbage hammock where I could see if he wandered off into the saw grass.

Then, when I'd hunted one area out, maybe I could move him to another hammock and do the same thing. The big problem, though, was how was I going to get my snakes down to Diamond Springs?

The white of the moon had come all the way across the shack floor and was halfway back again before I fell asleep, but when I woke in the morning it seemed like I hadn't slept at all.

After breakfast I put Dad on the log and washed off his shoes and put them on him, and then I took my snake stick and said good-bye and started off just like it was any other day.

But I went only a few hundred yards down the path, then circled back and laying in wait in a grove of scrub oak, watched. For a long time Dad just sat, only moving enough to stay in the sunlight.

I put my head down on my arms and the lazy hum of buzzing insects and the warmth of the sun creeping along the sand made me drowsy, and I felt my eyes closing. For a while I fought against the urge to sleep, but after my troubled and near sleepless night, I couldn't fight it, and drifted off.

I don't know how long I slept, but when I awoke it was with a start and the feeling that something terrible was about to happen. I lifted to my elbows and looked to the clearing. Dad was gone.

I jumped to my feet and in my haste ran only a few yards before stumbling and going over on my face. I was up in an instant and running again. In the clearing in front of the shack I stopped to look around, and when I couldn't see him, I started running toward Cypress Pond.

Instead of staying on the path which would have taken me through Piny Woods, I took a shortcut across a wide expanse of flat ground grown to knee-high grass.

Even before I got to the pond, I knew Dad was down there, because he had startled buzzards and several hawks, some terns and a whip of blackbirds, the eagle that sometimes fished there, and a number of lesser birds into the air, and they were circling and waiting for him to leave so they could come down again and be about their business of searching for food.

I ran swiftly until I hit the soft bottom and then was slowed to a mud-slogging walk. I looked for his fresh trail and spotted it a couple of hundred feet to my left. I angled over, and the muck sucked me down at every step, and I wondered how he had found the strength to get through it.

When I came to his trail, I followed where it angled in toward the water. His tracks disappeared ahead of me where a thick curtain of gray moss hung from a tree. I could see that he had fallen and that in some places he must have crawled for a distance on his hands and knees before pulling himself erect again.

Every inch of me wanted to hurry, but there was no help for that. Each step had to be a deliberate and difficult maneuver.

When I came to the moss, it was so thick I had to part it with my hands to pass through. Here his trail disappeared into the water, but I assumed he had gone straight on ahead. I stopped once to call out, and to look left and right through the trees, hoping to get a glimpse of him.

I should have known he wouldn't answer me, and when I couldn't see him I bent low to see if I could distinguish a mud trail where he had disturbed the bottom. But the water of Cypress Pond was so coppery, it wasn't likely a bottom disturbance would show on the surface.

I stood then and held my breath, hoping to hear him sloshing around among the trees. But all I could hear were the impatient cries of the circling birds above and a cricket somewhere behind me and a frog off to my right.

There was nothing for me to do except move straight ahead. The trees formed only a narrow band around the open water of the pond. Where the water deepened the tree growth ended, and there was about ten acres of flat water without vegetation to obscure vision.

The bottom was not so difficult now, and I could move faster. By the time I came to the edge of the timber, I was thigh-deep in water. I stepped out from beneath the trees and instantly saw him hanging to a shelf of roots, the knee of a cypress about a hundred feet to my left.

At the same moment that I saw him, I saw Old Ironhead cruising straight toward him. But if Dad was frightened of the swimming alligator, it wasn't evident. In fact, it looked to me that he was just waiting for the alligator, and that was what he had come to Cypress Pond for.

I stood like a statue as I was suddenly struck stupid by the thought that Dad was *hoping* the alligator would come to him, and that was the reason *why* he had come to the pond.

I was horrified by the thought of it. What a long, long way his sickness must have taken him down the dark road inside himself.

And Ironhead was willing that it should be this way. Some alligators are fearful, but not Ironhead. All his life, anything that came to Cypress Pond was his.

I screamed: "Dad! Dad! Run!"

But his eyes were fastened on Ironhead. He leaned there against the cypress only waiting, it seemed, to be pulled under into darkness.

And Ironhead was eager. He had lifted in the water until his long snout was almost clear. His eyes bulged like big knots on a scaly tree trunk. He never wavered, and not only was he following the scent line, but he could see Dad plainly waiting.

"Run, Dad! Run!" I screamed again, but only the birds screamed back, and Dad never moved nor did Ironhead swerve an inch.

I thought maybe I should grunt, but I knew that would never even get into Ironhead's brain. There was nothing to do except try to get to Dad, and I began splashing through the water so that it boiled into a froth of bubbles around me. Yet, hard as I pressed forward with my thighs and flailed the water with my hands, I could move only so fast, and I could see well enough that it wasn't fast enough to beat the alligator.

Anyone who hasn't seen an alligator swim wouldn't know how swiftly it can arrow along without more than a ripple cast back on each side. And when it has spotted its prey, there is no swerving left or right, and it comes in a direct line straight to the victim, because it knows it must get its teeth into a victim before it leaves the water, or all is lost.

When I could see that it was impossible to make it to Dad by running in the hip-deep water, I threw myself down and tried swimming. But I had on snake boots, and I couldn't move my legs fast enough to get up speed. I swam with an overhand stroke, flailing water until it flew and came back down like diamonds.

I had moved only a few feet when I was breathing hard. I skipped a stroke then, and dared to glance out toward Ironhead; I was so surprised to see he had stopped swimming that I let my feet sink to the bottom and stood up.

Apparently confused by the disturbance I was making in the water, the gator slowly swung its snout my way. When I saw this happening, I splashed all the harder. Slowly, as though trying to understand this unexpected development, Ironhead cruised to the left and to the right, as though trying to wind me.

I turned toward Dad and started yelling again: "Run, Dad! For God's sake, run!"

Who knows if my voice got through to him. His eyes were still riveted on the gator, and when he saw the gator was not coming he loosened his hold on the cypress knee and slowly started making his way through the trees back toward shore.

Then I turned my full attention on the gator, and at the same time Ironhead turned his full attention on me. There wasn't any doubt now about his intentions. He had winded me and decided that I was to be the victim. I encouraged him by splashing harder, and then wondered if I could avoid those jaws and slip around onto his back like Mr. Shen did when he wrestled gators.

"If one comes for you," Mr. Shen had said after an exhibition, "just remember that he can't get you except by attacking head-on. If you can get off to one side and then slip down around and ride him, you can whip him down. But look out for that tail! I've seen more than one man get all busted up by that tail!"

It looked easy the way Mr. Shen did it. It looked so easy no one would ever believe it might be dangerous. He'd get around any alligator as smooth as jelly on bread and wrap his arms and legs so tightly he looked like he was part of the beast.

When Ironhead was twenty feet out, and I was sure Dad had made it to safety, I began to retreat toward the trees. I wasn't going to ride him if I didn't have to.

In his eagerness, Ironhead was swimming high, and backing away I could see the scars along his back where poachers had tried to kill him with everything from spears to bullets. There was one large, curious cross-hatching that could only have been made by a machete. It sure marked him.

It was plain to see the gator was gaining on me. I'd never make it to high ground, that was certain. What also was apparent was the fact that I wasn't going to be able to wrestle him. I couldn't move fast enough through the water to get clear of those jaws and swing around on his back—I was certain of it!

It was a wonder that I wasn't too frightened to move. But there was no room for fright, only for flight. I couldn't afford to be scared. There would be time for that after . . . well, if there was an after.

Right now I had to get out or up . . . I dared to turn and look. Within five feet stood a cypress with its knees

44

knuckling up out of the water. It was that cypress or nothing, nothing. . . .

I turned completely away from the gator and, with visions of that great mouth gaping and those long teeth flashing in the sun, I flew through the water, wrapped both arms around the bulging roots, and with a grunt and all my strength hoisted myself onto the knobby wooden shelf. Even as I did, I thought I heard Ironhead's jaws snap shut, but it might have been the slap of my boots against the tree trunk.

With both arms around the trunk of the tree, I didn't dare turn around to see where the gator was, lest I fall back into the water. I leaned for several minutes trying to control my breathing.

When I could breathe easily again, my arms and legs began to tremble. I knew I had to control them or I'd fall back into the water. I made my mind force my limbs to stay steady, and as they did, I thought: "Old gator, you aren't the only ironhead around these parts."

Then slowly I began to maneuver a turn. Inch by inch I came sideways. Careful as a cat I turned my feet so the slippery boot soles wouldn't slide down the slippery shelf of roots. And I came around, all the way, until my back was flat to the tree trunk. Then I turned my eyes down.

The gator was still there. He was eying me like a snake eyes a bird it wants to come closer. Then he lifted, but not high enough, and fell back with a splash. He swam ten feet out and ten feet back. He swam around the tree half a dozen times. But he couldn't get me.

Then I thought of Dad, and I listened. But I couldn't hear him splashing around in the muck, and there was no noise except from the birds, who had been watching from their high place in the sky. For all I know, some of them had been hoping the gator would get me, because there would be plenty of scraps coming to the surface if he had, and then they, as well as Ironhead, would be well fed.

If Ironhead had any ideas of giving up, he gave no sign. Sometimes he'd swim out as far as thirty or more feet, but always he would return to cruise in circles.

Sometimes as I stood there on the narrow shelf of protruding roots braced against the tree trunk I got to thinking of how it might have all ended, and then I got scared all over and started trembling, and my mind would get busy and tell my legs to hold still.

The birds were the first to give up. One by one they gradually filtered back down out of the sky: the buzzards took up their watch on the tallest trees, the terns started swinging back and forth across the pond's surface looking for small fish, and a pair of hell-divers popped up from somewhere and looked me over from a safe distance.

Meanwhile I was stiffening, and I didn't know how much longer I could stand on the narrow, lumpy cypress knee. I could gradually feel my legs go dead under me, and I was sure that if the gator didn't give up soon, I'd be back in the water with him.

I thought about jumping when Ironhead was out

making a far swing. Perhaps I could make it to shallow enough water to discourage him from following. But I couldn't trust my legs. I couldn't feel them now, and if I jumped, they might collapse like noodles.

It must have been about noon, because the sun was staring straight down into the watery arena, when the gator swam right beneath me and lay there for a long, long look.

I stared back, and then like a log that has finally soaked up all the water it can hold, Ironhead slowly sank from sight.

I tried to see what direction he might take by watching for surface disturbance, but there was not a bubble or a ripple, and for all I knew he might be lying right below me on the bottom, waiting for me to come down.

I hung tight for what seemed like forever, but actually was probably no longer than fifteen minutes. Then I slid off the cypress knee and my legs folded under me, and I knelt on the pond bottom up to my chin in the water.

I stayed quiet for a few minutes watching the water for some sign. Then I reached up for the cypress and slowly pulled myself erect. Gradually I felt life flowing back into my legs. I took a step and then waited. I took another and another until I had put the tree between me and where the gator had submerged.

Still moving as quietly as the water would permit, I walked from tree to tree, pausing to lean on each. Then when the water was only knee-deep, I broke into a run and didn't stop until I was back in the saw grass.

I don't think I would have stopped even then, except I folded up like I was hollow and all the air had suddenly seeped out.

I lay there under the sun until I could feel the strength getting back to my mind as well as my body. Then I swung around to a sitting position and looked back toward where the waters of Cypress Pond glinted through narrow openings in the hanging moss.

I sat for a long time, and then slowly I got to my feet and started back toward the shack. I turned to the path because it was easier walking, and then I could see through the trees that Dad was on his log.

I went right on past him without saying a word, and I wondered if he even knew that I had been there or if he thought the gator just changed his mind about attacking. In the shack I put splinters in the stove and shoved the coffeepot over the flames. At this minute I needed coffee more than anything I could think of.

When it was hot I poured a cup and went back outside to sit with my back to the shack. I looked over at Dad, and then I knew that things had come to such a place in my life that I had to do something about them. Just dreaming and praying and hoping was out. I'd have to act. But not today. Today I would only sit on the ground and rest and rest and rest.

CHAPTER 5

Next morning the air was hot and heavy and the day was dull. No redbirds whistled, nor did a single quail call from the open ridge where seed grass grew. It was the proper sort of day for an execution, if there was need for one—and there was.

I had planned it before falling asleep. As I saw it, I didn't have a choice. I had to take each day as it came and solve each problem as it presented itself. One by one, one after another—like walking a trail, step by step.

And today was the day old Ironhead had to die.

Then, after I'd seen to that, I'd have to hike on into Evenset and get a padlock, staple, and hasp for the door. Then tomorrow I'd have to get on with my snake hunting, because that big snake was the key to everything, and our only way out to where I could get help so Dad could be cured.

49

Maybe yesterday I'd grown up. I didn't know. But Mother had once told me that growing up was nothing more than facing up. And facing up meant being able to look the truth straight in the face.

Well, I could look the truth straight in the face, and the truth was that things weren't going to straighten out just because I hoped they would. If they were going to straighten out, I'd have to make them straighten out, and I wasn't going to do it by catching little snakes and hiding back in Big Swampy.

The rifle was bundled with a lot of other things we'd brought back into the swamp and had no need for. It was on the low rafters, and when the breakfast dishes were away, I pulled the bundle down.

The rifle was wrapped in a tarp, and with it were several boxes of shells. It had never been brought down before because I was afraid shooting would attract people to our place, and since this was the time of year when all birds and animals were out of season and illegal, shots might bring the law looking.

But now, law or no law, noise or no noise, I had to put a bullet between old Ironhead's eyes because I could never be certain while we lived here that Dad might not wander back to Cypress Pond.

I wanted to get it done and over with fast, and then I wanted to get on into Evenset so I'd have tomorrow to give to hunting the big snake.

While I looked the gun over, I wondered how it would be leaving Big Swampy. If it hadn't been for Dad, I could have been happy here. To leave and go to some city would be real punishment. If I had to be perfectly honest and face up, I'd have to say that I had been enjoying roaming Big Swampy hunting snakes and pigs.

Ever since I'd started my dreaming, I'd always told myself that before I settled down I was going to take a year and really explore the Glades. I used to sit in school and stare out the window at a gray-bearded live oak and in my mind I'd take the trip starting at Lake Okeechobee, zigzagging south to the Tamiami Trail, and then crossing over to go on down to Dead Man's and Shark rivers, and then across to come up the east side. . . .

And I'd see the pelicans flying their formations just like I was there, and hear a bobcat squawling, and see snook hiding under mangrove roots and tarpon rolling silver in the ditches. . . .

I had been in a hurry to do it then, because I knew the Glades were dying, that high dikes and broad canals were siphoning off the water that was its life, and that it wouldn't be long before the Everglades, the country's finest warm-water wildlife area, would be no more.

My father told me. Mr. Shen said it was so. Doc Bellamy used to get mad about it, and then after he was through being mad, he'd shake his head and look sad. I knew a lot of the birds were becoming extinct, and that others were becoming scarce. I knew that game men were having a rough time hauling alligators out of one dried up sinkhole after another to ponds with water. Even I could see the changes. Ponds that had held water for more months of the year than they were dry, now were dry for more months than they held water. Even Mirror River was slowly sinking between its banks, and the old high-water mark was growing grass and trees.

That's why I would have liked to stay in Big Swampy, because I was afraid before I got such a chance again, Big Swampy would have become a desert of wire grass and little more.

But I put off the dream, because the rifle was in my hands and there was work to do. First I had to kill the gator, but my biggest job was getting the snake. Without that snake there wasn't even bus fare for the two of us, or any money to eat on while I was getting work, or any money to pay for Dad's treatment.

But killing the gator wasn't going to be easy, not for me. He had come to mean something, and I couldn't help thinking about how he liked lying in the sun warming himself, and then when he got hungry slipping off into the water and waiting patiently for an otter to make a mistake, or a fish to swim too close. . . .

I'd watched him often, and I'd grunted to him maybe a hundred times, and he always grunted back, though he knew I was no gator. He'd bellow for a fight and he'd wait and wait for a female, but he'd never get a fight or any female, because he was the only gator around.

In a way it didn't seem right for me to shoot him. We were the ones who should have moved. As it was, it seemed I was walking into a world in which I had no right to interfere. It was *his* world, not ours. *He was* Cypress Pond. *He was* Big Swampy. *He was* the Everglades.

He had a right . . . and it wasn't my place . . . oh! Baloney! What was I trying to sell myself, I wondered.

"Face up to it," I said aloud. Then I got up and shoved a box of shells into my pocket and went outside to where Dad was sitting on the log.

I sat down next to him and held out the gun. "It's a good gun," I said. "In perfect shape. If you keep a little grease on a gun and a little oil on the shells, they never get rusty. Good insurance, a little grease and a little oil."

My voice didn't sound right. It sounded like me imitating myself. So I shut up.

It is funny the things a fellow will do to delay getting at a piece of work. Now that I had decided to face up, I could see how all along I'd probably been putting off my real job.

Even my snake hunting was only a way for me to keep from facing up to the real problem. When I hunted snakes I could forget everything except snakes. If I went after pigs, I forgot everything except pigs. If I went to sit in the Piny Woods and grunt to Ironhead, I could forget about the shack and that Dad was sitting there looking off into space.

In a way I was as bad off as Dad. We were both running. Only it had been easy for me, because I liked the road I was running on, but Dad was all alone on some dark road inside himself and there weren't any snakes or pigs or herons or gators . . . only dark loneliness.

I could look forward to things like a trip to Diamond Springs or coming to the table to enjoy a meal. I'd be tired when I came to bed and I could stretch and stretch. I was warm and I was cold.

But Dad was always cold, even in the sun, and his eyes were cold as stones, and the veins on the backs of his hands were like blue ice . . . because he had nothing like a tomorrow to warm him.

I shook myself to get rid of the feeling like a horse shakes himself to get rid of flies.

"You stay here now, Dad," I said, as I got up and started toward the trail which led to the Piny Woods. "I won't be long."

The sun was trying to break through when I came to the dim trail at the edge of the pines. But it couldn't melt these clouds like it could a mist, because they were thick as cotton and the only help was the little breeze that had started tearing at them.

But it still was so muggy I was breathing hard long before I got to the stump where I'd sat so many times to grunt up Old Ironhead. And I was wet with sweat, and it wasn't the kind of sweating I like, the kind that pours out under a blazing sun. This was a sticky kind of sweating that doesn't dry and leave your skin fresh, but the kind of sweating that lies like oil.

A little way before the trail comes to the arrowhead of trees, there is a patch of scrub where some pig hunters must have cut trees at one time to make corrals.

The sun coming through brought the scrub up, and the trail goes around it. I was just starting on the turn when I heard some squealing, and then a litter of young pigs burst out into the open, and I thought, "What luck!"

My first impulse was to shoot one, but I decided that shooting Ironhead would make enough noise for one day, so I leaned the rifle carefully against a pine, and started slowly and carefully toward the pigs, which were standing spraddle-legged and stiff-tailed, looking at me.

They were fat-looking little fellows, and one of them would put just about enough meat on our table to tide us over until I could come by another snake and find some way to get it to Diamond Springs.

I heard the sow grunting somewhere in the scrub, but the pigs, long weaned, did not run toward her, but stood their ground. If they'd let me get close enough for a flying tackle, I'd have one by the leg, and then bleed it and carry it to camp for the cutting.

"Sowee. Sowee." I said it softly, but I could tell they'd never been hand fed, because at the sound of my voice each took a few quick jumps and then, poised for flight, turned to stare.

"Sowee. Sowee." I said it again, like a dove cooing, and this time the pigs didn't jump.

So I stood a moment letting them get accustomed to the sight and the smell of me. Then I took a few careful steps. If I'd have had a little corn in my pockets it would have been simple. Usually I carried some. If you throw a little corn and let them taste it, it isn't long before they come looking to see what pocket you keep it in.

"Sowee. Sowee." A few more steps, and then the sow broke cover and grunted at me as if to ask: "Where's the corn?" It was obvious she had been hand fed before, a stray from some ranch.

So long as the sow didn't run, I knew the pigs would stay around. So I called softly and walked closer, and the sow stood her ground watching me with tiny eyes to see when I was going to keep my promise, and the pigs looked from me to the sow, not knowing whether to run.

They backed a little, but they didn't turn from me, and when I was six feet off and debating whether to try a flying tackle, there was a crashing in the scrub and I turned to see the long, white tushes of a huge boar.

At the sound the pigs broke and ran, and the sow ambled off to one side grunting a protest, and I swung about to face the boar with nothing but my hands for protection, because there wasn't even time to go for my knife before the huge pig charged. It lowered its head to get an upward thrust, and as I dived to one side I heard my pants' leg rip as the boar went past.

Before the boar could turn to charge again, I was squirreling my way up a tree to where I could get a handhold on a branch and lift myself to safety. Seeing its quarry get away, the boar gave a squeal of rage and charged the tree.

I grabbed, got the branch, and in the same instant the boar clamped its teeth over the heel of my snake boot. When I lifted myself out of range, it was with one boot on and one boot off.

The boar rammed my boot into the ground and kept charging it as though it were a living thing. I'd never seen such an angry pig and guessed that perhaps it had been hunted by dog packs and probably been shot at more than once.

The slash pine I was in had no large branches to provide a comfortable roost. Most of them looked as though they would hardly hold my weight; I went a little higher so there'd be branches below in case the ones I was hanging to broke.

Having made a mess of my boot, the boar came to the tree trunk to look up. Its eyes were evil. Its tushes were hooked, and one was broken and had a ragged edge.

It was that tush which had torn my pants. I shivered a little when I thought of how close I had come to getting a leg cut out from under me.

I looked over to where the rifle leaned against a tree. It was a good ten trees or more away. If I'd had it, I would have dropped that boar right where he stood. Not that I wanted the meat. I'd eaten chops from swamp boars before, and they were so strong the only thing that would ever cure them was a month in vinegar and then a week in the smokehouse.

I think I'd have taken a chance and shot the pig anyway. Boars are always a threat. Especially boars that have once been hunted. And, in spite of their bulk, they can move as quiet as a mouse, and they are smart enough to double back along a trail and ambush a man.

Once a boar got a man down, he'd probably never get up. They could rip a man to pieces. I'd seen them kill dogs, and it wasn't pretty. What's more, they'd eat on a man or dog after they'd done with him.

Though my position in the tree wasn't a good one, I knew I was secure enough to wait the boar out. The delay would cut into my day, and I'd probably have to wait until tomorrow to go to Evenset for the lock.

Every once in awhile the boar would go down the trail as though to leave. Then he'd root around, throwing up sand, and suddenly come charging back to see if I was still there.

"Get out of here, pig!" I hollered at the boar. "Beat it."

At the sound of my voice the pig ran in circles around the tree and grunted frantically. Several times he attacked the tree itself as though to root it out so he could get at me.

I was getting arm-weary hanging there, with only about half my weight resting where I straddled a limb. But I figured the boar would tire before I did and run off to find the sow. It was a pretty good bet he was trailing along after her, waiting for her to come in season.

"Go find your old lady," I yelled, and the pig squealed and rammed into the tree. "Some other pig is going to get her if you don't," I warned the boar. Then he looked up at me as though trying to fathom the sound. "That's right," I said, "you'll be left out in the cold if you don't get going."

The boar shook his tushes and attacked the snake boot again, after which he looked up at me as though to plainly say: "Come down and I'll show you. Just put a leg where I can reach it."

Then almost as suddenly as the boar had burst on me, it wheeled and ran down the trail to disappear. I waited awhile and then slowly slid to the ground. I hadn't taken two steps in the direction of my rifle when the boar came crashing out of the underbrush.

I leaped for the nearest tree and yanked myself out of reach. "You devil!" I shouted. "You old devil!"

The boar had only circled and hid himself in the scrub, hoping I'd come down. If I'd been a foot farther away from that tree, he'd have gotten me.

Well, there was nothing to do now but wait the pig out. It was early in the day, and knowing pigs, I knew he would tire of waiting long before dark, and then I'd be able to come down.

I moved about from branch to branch until I was reasonably comfortable, and then just as I was about to turn my attention back to the boar, I thought I saw something move far back on the trail.

I swiveled around for a better look but could see nothing, so I thought perhaps it had been a bird flicking into an opening. I was about to turn back to the boar, and again I detected a hint of movement.

I parted some branches in front of me to see better, and then I got a glimpse of Dad coming down the trail straight to where the pig was waiting.

For a moment I couldn't even think. Then I was shouting loud as I could:

"No, Dad! Go back! Go back, Dad!"

But if he heard me he didn't heed, and he appeared and disappeared among the trees, but he was coming on the trail and the trail passed beneath me right where the boar stood.

CHAPTER 6

Roaming Big Swampy to hunt snakes had put me in some tight spots, but never had I been faced with an emergency like this.

When that boar winded Dad, he'd charge. The pig would knock him flat, and then before I could come down out of the tree, he'd be ripping him apart with those long tushes and his sharp teeth.

I tried to think, but my mind wouldn't work. Thoughts whirled around inside my head, one colliding with another. Then I got hold of myself.

I had to get that rifle. There was no other way. And, I had to get it fast.

I looked down the trail again. Dad was walking slowly as though heavily burdened. He was bent forward, his shoulders were hunched, and his eyes were straight to the ground where he put one foot and then the other slowly on the dim trail. If he had looked up, perhaps he'd have gotten a glimpse of the boar. I shouted again:

"Dad! Dad! There's a wild boar on the trail. Dad, turn back!"

He never even lifted his head. My eyes scanned the earth as though searching for clues and then came to rest on the battered snake boot. Maybe, just maybe, it would work. In an instant I had the other boot off, and waving it so the boar could see it, I threw it down the trail. When it hit the ground the boar was on it, and in that second I was out of the tree and running.

But the boar turned in a flash, and before I could get to the rifle he had sent me up another tree.

I was as wet with sweat as though I'd been standing in the rain. It came down off my forehead into my eyes to blind me. It made my hands so slippery I had a hard time hanging on.

I tore off my shirt, balled it up, and threw it down the trail. The boar took after it like he had the boot.

Again I slipped out of the tree and was running. But again the boar swung and as swift as a deer was after me. I had to climb another tree. But now I wasn't more than a few feet from the rifle. I took two seconds to scrub the sweat out of my eyes, and saw that Dad was still coming down the trail.

I had only my pants left, and I was sure I couldn't get them off in time. I thought of my knife, pulled it from the sheath, and in desperation aimed at the pig's eyes. The blade only grazed the pig's head, and he shook as though to dislodge a fly and gave an angry squeal.

Then I thought to yank off my belt. I swung it low so the boar could reach it. Then I flung it and the pig followed.

The instant the boar's back was turned, I was down out of the tree and running. I had the rifle and turned. The boar was coming back in a swift gallop, grunting every time his short legs hit the ground.

I leaned against the tree and threw up the gun. Maybe I had half a second to say to myself: "One shot. That's all. One shot."

I was scared. My knees were weak. The charging boar was all mixed up with the trees and grass and the scrub behind him. The woods seemed to reel and to stagger. Then suddenly everything came into focus.

It was like a miracle. I'd heard of things like that, when adrenaline gets into a guy's blood stream and gives him extra strength. Soldiers especially have told stories of how they were so frightened they couldn't concentrate on pulling the trigger, and then all at once something inside gave them the will to do it.

It was like that with me. I could feel the energy surge through me, and then the pig's head was clear and right there. The sight on the front of the rifle barrel fell smoothly into the notch of the rear sight. I leaned against the tree with one shoulder and squeezed the shot off as smoothly as though I had been shooting at a harmless squirrel.

Everything was so sharp I could even see the bristles on the boar's head, and I saw the tiny hole suddenly appear as the boar grunted and went to his knees.

I sidestepped behind the tree, and the boar went

past me on his knees, making the sand fly. Two steps beyond me he rolled over, kicked a few times with his stout little legs, and then lay quiet. There was only a small trickle of blood where the bullet went in. Nothing else. Nothing.

Then the weakness swept over me. I dropped the rifle and grabbed the tree to keep from falling. I was sick to my stomach. The rough bark of the tree scraped my cheek, and I could smell the turpentine as I slid to a sitting position.

Then I thought about Dad and turned to look. He had turned and was going back. Having seen me, he must have known I would stop him. I let him go.

I sat until I felt better. Then I got up and picked up the rifle. The breeze was stronger and it was drying the sweat, and the cottony clouds were clearing the sky. I began gathering up my things—shirt, belt, knife, and boots.

The boots had gotten the worst of it but were still wearable, so I slipped them on. The shirt had a long tear, but I wore it. Looking down at my clothing, I saw I was something less than well dressed. I shrugged.

The buzzards were already gathering. I suppose I should have cut off a chunk of that boar, because we certainly could've used the meat—strong or not. But I couldn't bring myself to touch him. I looked up at the big birds circling just above the treetops and thought to myself: "You can have him."

Then I started wearily back up the trail toward the shack. Dad was on his log when I got back, and when I went by I said: "That was a close one, don't you think?"

But I doubt that he even saw the boar. I think he probably spotted me on the trail, and knowing that I would turn him back, he had voluntarily returned.

I went past him and into the shack and put a few pine slivers into the stove and lighted them and shoved the breakfast coffee close to the flames.

I drank a lot of coffee, though I'd never liked it until we moved into Big Swampy. Now it sure was a comfort. It woke me in the morning, picked me up when I was feeling low, and after I'd had a rough time, it seemed to soothe my nerves and give me enough steam to get going again.

I poured Dad a cup when it was hot, and I loaded both cups with sugar for energy. Taking the tin cups outside, I handed one to Dad and then put my back to the shack to sit and think about what I had to do next.

The sun was directly overhead, so I had the afternoon ahead of me. Perhaps, I thought, it would be better to try for Ironhead at night. I could bring him much closer in the dark, and then I could turn on the jack light and get him right in his little brain box, and there would be less chance of wounding him and making the job of hunting him down to finish him off a really tough one. Perhaps I should go into Evenset and get the padlock, staple, and hasp. But what to do about Dad?

I couldn't leave him alone. He seemed intent on

keeping his date at Cypress Pond with Ironhead. I had to suppose he was on his way there this morning when he came down the trail while the boar had me up the tree.

Perhaps I could nail the door and the two windows of the shack shut. It would be quite a job, and then I'd have to tear them open when I got back.

Maybe I could take him with me as far as the edge of town, and then leave him and hurry to get what I needed, and get back before he wandered too far.

That seemed to be the best way. It might even do him good to go for a long walk. He sat so much his muscles were withering.

Getting up, I took my cup inside and then changed to my other shirt and pants. The beat-up snake boots would have to do, because I had no others.

Dad was sipping the last of his coffee when I came back outside. I took the cup from him and said: "We're going to take a walk, Dad. I want you to come along."

I sat his cup on a nearby stump and took him by the arm. He got up and we struck out north along the edge of a sandy rise in the ground because there was less brush and the footing was fairly solid.

For a while I kept a hold on Dad's arm. Then I let go and moved out ahead. He got the idea and followed along. I wanted to hurry, but I held back so Dad could stay with me. He shuffled instead of lifting his feet, and the going was slow.

It didn't matter, because we weren't more than six miles from Evenset, and alone I could make it walking fast in an hour and a half, and with Dad I figured it would take closer to two or maybe two and a half hours.

Every once in awhile I'd stop and sink to the ground to rest. I'd say: "Dad, sit down." But he'd just stand there waiting.

At times like that I wondered what was going through his mind, and if it would ever again find the right road so he could come around to being like he used to be.

Sometimes as I looked at him I wondered if the hospital really could work a cure. Even if I had the money and got him where special doctors could work with him, would he come out of it?

Maybe I ought to go to Doc and just tell him that I didn't know what to do any more. If I'd only had the money! But I didn't, so what was the use of thinking about it, and I just didn't dare take a chance on his being sent to The Institution.

It wasn't quite so hot now with a breeze blowing, and Dad seemed to be standing up real well. He just moved along at his steady pace without looking up or around at anything, and I thought that the wonderful muscles he once had had must still have something in them or he wouldn't have been able to walk so far.

As soon as I could see the church steeple, I stopped. Then I looked around for a log, and I took Dad by the arm and led him over to it.

"You stay here, Dad," I said. "I won't be gone more than fifteen, twenty minutes, and then I'll be back. Now don't move, whatever you do."

If he did move, I didn't figure he could go far and I could find him easily. We were in a pine woods and there wasn't any scrub, and I could see for a good distance. He was tired, and I knew he'd sit for a while.

One thing was for sure, I'd have to dodge people I knew, and that meant almost everybody. But I could say that I was in a hurry, and that I was sorry, but I'd have to keep going. Then if they asked how Duke was, I'd say "fine."

If there was one thing I didn't want, it was to have the people around Evenset really know how it was with Dad. I'd seen how they had treated Dummy Bergen and even old Mrs. Trimble, who had two cows and sold milk.

The kids had been especially mean. They'd called her Crazy Trimble, and sometimes a gang had gotten together to go out to her place and throw stones on the roof and shout:

"Come out! Come out, you crazy old witch!"

Then when she'd step onto the porch, they'd squeal and holler and run, and even some of the town girls went with the boys.

And they'd always be tripping up Dummy, or asking him questions like: "How's the rocks rattling in your head today, Dummy? Pretty good?"

Kids could be mean, and I didn't aim to have them poking fun at Duke Doucette. Dad had always been a sort of hero around town. He had known everybody and everybody always wanted to stop and talk with him. The boys especially came over, and he'd let them sit behind the wheel of his big truck, and he'd open the hood so they could see the powerful engine. So now, to have these same kids see him, the way he was—I couldn't face it!

At the edge of town I stopped and looked up the street. There were only a few people walking along the side of the road, so I started out fast and with my head down.

I got all the way to Winnie Dean's store without having to look up or say hello to anyone. I looked through the window of the store and didn't see anyone, so I walked in. The bell above the door rang as I closed it, and Winnie Dean, dressed as always in the same faded blue dress, came out from behind the curtains that hid the room in which she lived.

At first, looking against the light, she didn't recognize me. Only after I said that I needed a hasp, staple, and a padlock did she say:

"Well, darn! Doug Doucette! Where you been, boy? And where's that handsome father of yours?"

"Oh, we moved to near Immokalee," I lied.

"Dad back driving truck again?" she asked.

"Yes, he's driving again," I said.

She went to a bin along the wall and began pawing through assorted hardware. "Well, here's a hasp and here's a staple to go with it," she said. Then she went to the other wall and took down a padlock with a key in it.

"Who you going to lock up?" she asked.

For a minute I was off balance, then I knew she was

just making conversation, so I said: "Well, I thought I'd lock Dad in nights so he doesn't go around chasing the girls." Then I laughed.

"I believe it. I believe it." Mrs. Dean thought it was a great joke.

"How much?" I asked.

"That'll be two dollars," she said, and if it had been any more I wouldn't have been able to pay, because two dollars was exactly what I had. When she started to put them in a bag, I said:

"I'll just stick them in my pocket, Mrs. Dean."

"Okay, boy," she said, handing me the hardware. I backed toward the door sort of bowing a little, and said:

"Thank you, Mrs. Dean. Thank you and good-bye."

She squinted against the light from the door and said: "Say hello to that handsome father of yours. Tell him we miss him around here."

"I sure will," I said. "I sure will." And then I was outside and the door was closed.

I turned and started trotting, but then held myself down to a walk and went back up the street. I was almost at the edge of town when a new copper-colored Chevy came off a side street; I recognized it as Doc Bellamy's.

I put my head down, hunched my shoulders, and hoped Doc wouldn't see me. But when I heard the tires scuffing sand, I knew that he had, and that he was stopping.

"Doug," he called, and I had to turn around. "Well,

Doug, I thought it was you. Say, it sure is good to see you." And Doc meant it. His wrinkles around his eyes and his mouth smiled at me, and I had to be polite.

"It's nice to see you, Doc," I said. "Mighty nice."

"How's your dad?" he asked.

"Oh, Dad is fine," I said.

"Then he came out of it?" He made it a question. I nodded. "I figured he would," Doc went on. "Man as strong as Duke Doucette couldn't stay in a state of shock forever. Did he get well real easy, or did something scare him into it?"

"Real easy. It came real easy," I said.

"Where you living?" Doc asked.

I told him what I had told Winnie Dean, that we were living near Immokalee, and that Dad was driving truck again.

"But why Immokalee?" Doc asked. "This was always your dad's home."

"I don't know . . . I suppose . . . I think. . . ." I stammered and Doc interrupted:

"Maybe he wanted to get away from things that would make him remember," Doc said.

"Yes, that's it," I said, but I knew I'd said it too fast, like I was grabbing at a straw he had offered me.

"Well, that's best sometimes," Doc said, but now the wrinkles around his eyes and on his forehead were of the asking kind.

"I have to hurry, Doc," I said, and I turned and started down the road.

Doc started to ask me what I was doing way up here

in Evenset, and then he stopped talking and only said: "Well, good luck, Doug, and remember me to your father."

I didn't turn around, and only said: "Good-bye, Doc. I'll sure tell Dad."

Before I reached the edge of town I heard his car start up, and I heard the tires scuff sand as he drove down the street.

Dad was right where I'd left him, and that was a relief. I had been afraid he might get the notion to go into town.

"Come on, Dad," I said. "We're going back home." And we started back down the trail, me out front and Dad trailing behind like a big, obedient dog.

CHAPTER 7

It was sundown before I got the hasp screwed to the doorjamb and the staple screwed to the door. Then to the outside of both windows I nailed tough pine limbs across like bars, so the sun and wind could get in but nobody could get out. I figured that would hold him, but I wondered if inside himself he would be hurt by it.

Maybe he was still enough alive to things to know that he was being locked up like an animal. I looked over to where he was sitting, but I couldn't think of anything else to do, so I just hardened myself to the whole business.

Then I turned my attention to the possum I'd knocked out of a tree in a deserted ranch clearing on my way home from town. I skinned it and cut it up and put it on to boil. I put in a bay leaf and a little vinegar and sugar to make it sweet-sour. Then I got out some rice and made ready for a supper of possum and rice.

The possum was a young one, and would boil tender in a half hour, but even so, it was dark by the time we sat in the circle of lamplight to eat.

The possum was just right. The sweet-sour flavor had my mouth watering even before I sat down, and it was as good as it smelled. I even thought Dad ate with a little more enthusiasm than usual.

As soon as we'd cleaned up the rice and meat and sucked the bones, I cleared the table and helped Dad to bed. Then I took the rifle and the jack light and went outside and closed the door and snapped on the lock.

At least now I wouldn't have to worry that Dad was going to roam off somewhere.

At the edge of the clearing I stopped and closed my eyes. I kept them closed for about a minute, and then when I opened them I could see better. Trunks of the trees came into good focus, and the brush was visible for a long way down the trail.

I often wished I had eyes like an owl that could let in enough light to see more plainly at night. I noticed, though, that the more often and the longer I stayed in the dark, the better I could see. I noticed too, that it wasn't all in just seeing, but in recognizing what I saw.

Like a lump on a limb. I could tell in an instant it was a hooty owl by the shape. Or a dark shadow above the saw grass. I could tell it was a deer's head in a second by the ears. Or a possum in a tree. I knew it was no mistletoe because there was a tail, usually hanging.

Seeing in the Glades is like that. It isn't that one man's eyes are better than another's. It is only that one man is alert to what he is likely to see, while another wouldn't know what he was looking at even if it was right in front of his nose.

I was thinking like that as I walked down the trail to keep my mind off how I was going to kill Ironhead. After this day was over, I thought, it will probably be a day I'll never forget. Already more had happened than sometimes happens in a month.

There was no moon—it would rise later—but the stars gave good light. But I didn't need the light, because I could pick out landmarks, and when I came to the patch of scrub where I'd killed the boar, I heard a scuttling in the brush and saw a shadow shoot away, and I figured a bobcat had been feeding.

I didn't want to go near the boar, so I left the trail and went around the place where it lay, and then I came back on the trail. I don't know what it was about that boar, but I had a feeling it was like something evil creeping up on me—even now, after it was dead. I knew it was nonsense, but the way it had tried to ambush me and then cut me down without warning—well, I just wanted no part of it.

When I came to the stump I sat down on it and leaned my gun against the side. I thought I'd do some grunting from here to get Ironhead started, and then go to the shore to finish it off.

Across the clearing the dark rise of trees marked Cypress Pond. I could make out individual trees because they stood above the others, and because I had sat for so many nights on the stump that I'd even gotten to identifying individual clumps of grass around me.

I cupped my hands to my mouth and made a horn and from deep down in my throat came up with a "Whuuuump." I waited, cupped my hands again, and went: "Whuuuump. Whuuuump. Whuuuump."

Then I put my hands down and felt for the gun. It was standing there just where I'd put it, and somehow I was surprised that it was. I don't know why, unless I had expected that it might vanish into air, that none of what happened today or what was going to happen tonight was true.

Old Ironhead didn't answer. All I heard was a coon squawling somewhere off on a cabbage hammock, and some crickets back of me in the dead wood of Piny Woods, and a few frogs trying to get a beat going, but not doing very well because it was pretty far along in the season for them. They'd start a chorus, but it would quickly cut out just as though every frog had been given a separate signal at the same time to shut up. Then one or two or half a dozen would sing softly and more would join in, until the gang was in voice and—bang—just like that they'd be silent.

I called out in a half grunt and half bellow half a dozen times and then sat listening. I could actually feel my ears pick up just a little to catch the answering "whuuuump" of the gator, but it didn't come.

That was strange, because Ironhead had never failed me before, not in a hundred times when I had come to sit in the Piny Woods and "Whuuuump" him up for a little company.

Maybe he'd found a female, but I didn't believe it. Or maybe he was down in his damp, dark cave under the tree roots. But, why, on a warm night like this?

I waited awhile and saw several hooty owls following in shadowy single file from the Piny Woods across the clearing, which was brighter because the starlight could shine there. They disappeared into the dark rise that was the woods around Cypress Pond.

The coon squawled again, and it sounded like a young one that was in trouble. Maybe a snake had grabbed it, and maybe the snake wasn't big enough to swallow the coon, and the coon was squawling while the poison took effect. I didn't think so. Snakes shouldn't be out.

Maybe a couple of hooty owls had caught the young coon out in a clearing and were taking turns attacking it, hoping to get in enough licks with their talons to keep it from reaching a hole in a hollow tree. But where was the old coon? She should have been with her young.

I "whuuuumped" once more from the stump, and then when there was no answer I got down and picked up the gun and walked through the saw grass across the clearing to the trees. I saw the open wedge among the trees where I could come to open water without hardly getting my feet wet.

As I came to soft ground that squished underfoot, there was a swishing of wings and a crackling of branches and the squawking of the black capped night herons. They were frightened from their night camp.

I stood still waiting until the birds were clear of the trees, so the noise of them wouldn't interfere with my hearing. Then I walked ankle-deep into the water.

"Whuuuump. Whuuuump. Whuuuump." I offered Ironhead another invitation. But he did not accept.

In a way I felt relieved. Now with a lock on the door maybe I wouldn't have to kill the gator after all. I surely had no stomach for it, but I wondered if I could ever be at peace knowing that Ironhead was lying down there—lock or no lock. I waited a little longer and then decided to call it a night, so I took the trail and hit back to the shack and went to bed.

The next morning I stirred the grits and poured Dad a cup of coffee. Then I said, "Come on now," and I went over and touched his arm. He shuffled his legs to the side of the bunk and slid them to the floor. I helped him up and helped him dress. Then he sat and looked at his coffee while it was cooling.

"You're going to have to stay inside today," I told him. His expression didn't change. I spooned some grits onto the tin plates and went out and got the butter.

After we ate I took Dad by the arm and steered him outside and let him wander down the trail to the outhouse while I cleaned up the shack and straightened the blankets on the bunks. When I went outside Dad was on the log. I let him sit a little while and cleaned some of the sand off the rifle. I opened the action, saw there was no sand inside, and then closed it again.

Then I poured myself another cup of coffee to give Dad a few more minutes before locking him up.

When the coffee was gone, I led Dad inside, and then I closed the door, slapped on the lock, and snapped it shut. I didn't like the sound. So I turned away quickly and swung out onto the trail and headed for Cypress Pond.

I would give myself only a couple of hours at the pond, and then I was going to head out and hunt for the snake.

When I came to the stump I sat and grunted, but like last night, there was no answer. Then I walked toward the water, and birds began leaving the trees until the air was full of feathers. I had never seen so many birds around Cypress Pond before. I wondered why. Something surely had attracted them. But I couldn't see anything. Yet I was certain there had to be something. There were three and four times the number of birds the pond could support.

Well, birds or no birds, I was looking for a gator. I walked ankle-deep into the water, where I could get an unobstructed view of the entire pond and "whuuuumped" again. I neither heard nor saw Ironhead.

So I went back to high ground and started to circle to where I knew his cave went deep beneath cypress roots. As I moved, hundreds of birds took off out of the trees and off the water ahead of me, while hundreds of others settled back down behind.

I found fresh pig tracks and figured it was the sow and her litter. Two deer had come to drink, and by the size of the tracks I judged them to be a doe and her fawn. There were coon and possum tracks, and a bobcat had come along hunting and killed a coot, judging from the feathers, and then hiked with it to higher ground to feast.

At intervals along the pond edge I walked a little way into the water to have a look at the pond surface, hoping the gator had come out. But there was no sign of him, and then when I came opposite his lair, I knew why.

There in the mud and along the higher ground in the saw grass was his trail. He had moved out, left Cypress Pond.

At first I couldn't believe it. Why should a gator who had probably lived all his life in the pond want to leave? He'd never find another pond with as much food or that was as exclusively his. He was lucky if he found another pond that kept its water all year.

Maybe he was headed for the river. I'd always had the feeling that wild things, even though they'd never been any place except where they were born, had a knowledge of the land that lay around them. I felt they knew about rivers and other ponds just from the way the land lay. I felt they knew about the sand dunes and the pine forests and the flats of saw grass and the cabbage hammocks without ever having gone out and toured the country to see them.

Maybe I was wrong, but it seemed that they knew. And now, I had a hunch, Ironhead was headed for the river.

But why?

The old gator couldn't possibly have known that I'd been coming to kill him.

Or could he?

I laughed at myself for thinking it. I wasn't superstitious, and though I'd heard the tales from Negroes at Evenset about how a dog could know when a man was dying and start howling days before the man even got sick, and I'd heard them claim an alligator could know you were out to get its hide even before you knew it yourself. . . .

It was silly, of course. How could animals know what a man thought even before the man knew about it?

But I'd heard strange tales about how gators would never touch a Seminole Indian because the spirits that protected the Indian would be sure to come back to get the gator. And you never heard about an Indian getting caught by a gator. White or black men, but not Indians!

There were stories too about how a gator knew days ahead that a pond was going to dry up and got out while the getting was good. But it couldn't be true, because game men were forever rescuing gators from dried up water holes and moving them to water.

Yet something had made that gator move, and if it was something I couldn't explain, maybe it was something there was no explanation for.

I followed the wide trail to a small pond, but the gator had only gone into the water to wet himself, then had crawled out and continued. I followed to where he had wallowed in a mud hole, but obviously he hadn't stayed long. Then where the trail turned toward the

81

river, I decided there was no point in following. Already I had spent so much time on the trail the day was shot, and I'd have no time to hunt for the big snake.

It was something of a relief not to have to kill the old guy, but I was going to miss him anyway. He'd been a comforting part of my life—so sufficient all by himself, lord and ruler of Cypress Pond, which was his whole world.

Maybe he knew the Glades were doomed. Maybe he was hitting for the river because Cypress Pond was due to dry up. I couldn't believe it. The pond had always held water, and the level had remained constant.

But I'd heard stories of mass migrations of animals and birds when a drought was due to hit a country, or when a crop of nuts failed to ripen, or when an animal the meat eaters depended on for food was about to be stricken by disease. . . .

But how could they know?

Well, I had more important things to attend to than the strange ways of animals and birds. So I swung back toward Cypress Pond and on passing along the shore was stopped in my tracks.

The water was dropping!

At first I thought I must be mistaken. But closer examination proved I wasn't. The high-water mark was plain to see on every cypress knee. Where I had stood in ankle-deep water, I could now stand on damp but naked land. Since I had tried to "whuuuump" Old Ironhead up the night before, the pond had dropped a good twelve inches. I could almost see the water running away.

I got a strange and frightening feeling, standing there watching the water pour itself away into some dark and mysterious place underground. The birds had known. They had come. Ironhead had known. He had gotten out.

Somewhere along the pond basin, the bottom had finally crumbled and given way as it had in other ponds in the Glades. Now Cypress Pond was losing its life, pouring it into some underground river that was perhaps giving life to another pond or taking the long and dark route to the sea.

Seeing it happen to lesser ponds had not stirred me. But to have it happen to something as enduring as Cypress Pond gave me the feeling that you couldn't depend on anything any more, not anything.

CHAPTER 8

✖ I didn't have to go down to Cypress Pond in the morning to know that it was without water. It seemed every bird in Big Swampy and maybe all the Glades had come to feast on the fish, snails, and water insects that were uncovered and left to die. I heard the birds even before I swung my feet out of bed to the shack floor.

I went outside in my shorts and walked a little way to where I could see through the trees, and the air above the pond was swirling with birds of every size and color; it was amazing how they kept from colliding.

I went back into the shack and said to Dad: "Cypress Pond went dry during the night. Every bird in Big Swampy is down there now filling its gullet."

After we'd eaten I gave myself a half-hour to have a look. The sun was only a little way up, but when I came to the shore there was such a wild winging that the lift of birds was like a cloud with its shadow over everything.

The screaming of the birds was so loud it seemed the leaves of a live oak vibrated from the sound. When I peered out through the trees into the muddy saucer, there were two otters feeding and a bobcat scooted for cover. I saw three coons and a dozen possum, but mostly there were birds.

I knew that even before sunset they would have the pond basin cleaned out, and there would be nothing except the skeletons of big fish, white and ribbed and long in the starlight—that's all that would be left of Cypress Pond.

Well, it was a cinch that wise old gator, that Old Ironhead, had known the plug was about to be pulled. There could be no other reason for his overland retreat. Alligators aren't given to wandering off like that, especially if they have to cross dry land. That gator had known when to make a move.

Well, it was the way of things, especially in the Glades. One pond disappeared and then another would appear. The whole peninsula was probably full of sinkholes, and when the limestone finally crumbled, the bottom just dropped right out of the hole and the water worked its way to some main stream or maybe just spread and sifted south.

It was no wonder, I thought, that some of the Negroes and Indians believed the Glades were haunted. For that matter, some white men thought so too. It isn't every day a man sees a lake disappear or another one appear. And it isn't every day that a sinkhole just fresh with water was filled with fish too.

I could see where it would be easy to believe that spirits might have a hand in such doings.

I waded through the muck a little way and picked up two small trout that the birds hadn't yet pecked on. They'd make our supper. I wondered how many fish had gotten away, gone underground with the water. It didn't seem likely that many had made it. There were some trout, already partly eaten, that looked like they'd weigh fifteen pounds. In some low holes the bream were layer on layer. The bottom crawled with insects, and bloodsuckers almost as big as my hand were waving their leathery tails and heads, looking for something to latch on to.

Finally I turned away and went back to the shack. The birds screamed their joy at my departure. Now they could get on with their feeding.

In the shack clearing I spilled the guts out of the trout and put them in the butter hole and covered it with palmetto. They'd keep until evening.

Dad was on the log, so I had to take him back inside, and then getting several sacks, I went out and snapped the lock on the door.

The sun had burned off the little mist that had been hanging in some of the low places, and it looked like it might be a smoking hot day. Well, I could take the heat. It didn't bother me, and if I looked in the right places, it would be a good day for snakes.

If I didn't find the big one—and the way things were

going, I was sort of thinking my luck wouldn't let me —maybe I'd get at least a three- or four-footer so I'd have something in the "bank" when the groceries ran out.

The "bank" was a deep, dark hole. I'd put the snake, bag and all, into it and cover it well. In the dark snakes usually stayed still. Rattlers are very sensitive and don't live long in captivity, even under ideal conditions. This way it would be in good shape at least until I had a chance to make a run for it to Diamond Springs.

I had hardly hit the side trail that ran a little way toward where I'd seen the big snake, when I startled a four-footer and it coiled and rattled at me, and I said to myself:

"Well, welcome little snake. You look to me like a good supply of rice and grits."

And that made me feel better, and I thought that maybe my luck hadn't all run out. I popped the snake into one bag and hadn't taken another dozen steps when there was another four-footer. I figured that maybe it was the first snake's mate. It didn't coil, but tried to run for it, so I put the forked stick in back of its head, got a good grip with my free hand, and slid it into the second sack.

It was like walking through the woods and finding a tree with money hanging on it.

It made me feel so much better that I sat right down to give myself a rest. Two snakes! And the sun wasn't hardly high enough to get into the shadowy places.

But now what? Well, I thought, the really smart

thing would be to take those two snakes straight to Diamond Springs. That would mean delaying the hunt for the big one, but with eight dollars I could go a long time and not get edgy about finding something so we could eat.

I knew I'd have to hitchhike. So I swung back along the offshoot trail to where I'd made my own trail, on down to the highway. I'd been over it enough so it was good walking. In the beginning I'd hacked away a lot of scrub, and now even a city guy could follow it in the dark.

But even though the trail was easy, I dripped with sweat. The sun was so hot it had burned the sky from a morning blue to a glassy white. I sure hoped Old Ironhead had made it to the river. If he'd got caught traveling on a day like this, there was no telling whether he'd make it. It was a blistering morning.

Dad would be better off in the shack than out on the log. At least he'd be in the shade. If he was on the log he moved along with the sunlight, no matter how hot it got.

When I came to the road I crossed over to the right side and lay back on an elbow under a scrub oak. The highway was dancing in heat waves, and there was a regular mirage down the road: castles with chimneys that were smoking heat right up into the sky.

When a car went by its tires were so hot I could hear the soft rubber sucking at the road, like it wanted to melt itself right down into the concrete. I got up each time a car came in sight to give it an easy motion south with my thumb, but they all just whizzed right on by.

When the sun got over to the afternoon side of the day I thought maybe I wasn't going to get a lift, and then a car pulled over and it was Mr. Bowles.

"Hey!" he shouted, as the tires skidded a little in the sandy shoulder. "This is lucky. I'm early this week. Didn't think I'd get to see you."

I laughed, because my luck was holding, and putting the snakes on the back seat, slid in beside him. He wiped his face with a huge, white handkerchief and said, "Whewww! Man! This is hot weather even for a Cracker."

I wiped my face on the sleeve of my shirt and said, "Thought I'd melt right on away."

He put the handkerchief away and then stepped on the gas, and the tires were licking along the concrete like they'd gone soft with the heat and it was a smooth ride.

"Got two, eh?" Mr. Bowles asked.

"Yeah. Just like that. Both together. Never been so lucky. I'm lucky all the way around today."

I felt like telling him about the big snake, but I wasn't that sure yet that he might not speak of it to someone and then the word would get around.

"You live alone back there?" he asked.

I hesitated, and then said: "No, my dad is with me."

"What's he do?"

"Well, he used to drive a truck, but now he's just sort of taking a little vacation between jobs." I looked at Mr. Bowles and thought I ought to dress it up a little more. "We like to go off like that once in awhile, and bach it. I catch snakes and a pig once in awhile, and he mostly fishes or sits in the shade and has himself a good rest. Driving truck, being on the road all the time, for a big trucking outfit, is pretty tough."

Mr. Bowles turned to me. "Don't I know it," he said. Then he put his eyes back on the road, but kept talking. "Seems like all I do is drive. Like today. Got a rush order from a new laboratory, so I have to make the trip myself."

Then we were quiet, and he pressed on the gas and the speedometer needle showed eighty and kept creeping up. The wind whipped around our faces, but it did nothing to cool us, because the air coming off the road was a hot as any coming out of a stove. The car started to heat up, and the heat gauge crept near the red danger mark, so he eased up on the gas until we were doing sixty, and there he held it and we hummed along.

It was too hot to even talk, so we didn't say anything more, and then we were coasting in through the gate under the big archway of the Diamond Springs Reptile Institute.

I got out of the car in front of the office building and thanked Mr. Bowles. Then I took the snakes off the back seat and went around to get my slip to collect the eight dollars.

The slip got damp and wilted just carrying it, but when I went into the main office it was air-conditioned, and it was like stepping from a furnace into a refrigerator, and I shivered and goose bumps sprouted on my arms.

The girl at the desk took the slip and went to the

cash register to get eight dollars. Before she came back, Mr. Shen, in his quick way, popped out of an office at the rear of the big room and called to me: "Got a minute, Doug? I'd like to see you."

I said "Sure," and when the girl handed me the eight dollars, she swung the half-door open for me and I walked between the desks and typewriters back to the door marked: DON SHEN.

It was partly open, but I waited anyway, and then he called: "Come on in, Doug." Mr. Bowles was in the office, and he was paring at a fingernail with a tiny pearl-handled knife.

"Sit down, Doug," Mr. Shen said, and I took the chair he pointed to. Then he put his hands into his lap, leaned back, and looked straight at me.

"You know a doctor by the name of Bellamy?" he asked.

I was no more prepared for the question than I would have been prepared to catch that big snake if it had suddenly appeared on Mr. Shen's desk. I couldn't answer.

"Well, it is obvious that you do know him," Mr. Shen said. Then he quickly added: "There's nothing to be afraid of. Nobody is after you for anything."

I swallowed, took a deep breath, and started to get hold of myself. Then I said: "Sure I know Doc Bellamy. He's from my home town."

It came to me that maybe Doc had only been visiting the Institute and that in one way or another my name had been mentioned in connection with snakes, and that Mr. Shen had told him that I sold snakes, and then

Doc would have acted surprised and said: "Well, what do you think of that! I know Doug Doucette and his dad real well. They're patients of mine, come from the same town."

Except I could tell right off from the next question that it wasn't quite like that. "Doc was wondering," Mr. Shen said, "where you and your dad were living."

"Oh?" I made it a question.

"Yeah. He just left a few minutes before you came in. Said he was worried about you and your dad, but didn't know where to look for you. Figured maybe you were catching and selling snakes, so he drove over to see if I knew anything."

I stayed quiet, and I noticed Mr. Bowles had stopped paring his fingernail and was looking at me as though he too wanted to hear what I would say. I let a good time pass, and then I said: "Well, that sure was nice of Doc. If you see him again tell him we're just sort of taking a vacation, baching it until Dad feels like going to work again."

I had to tell Mr. Shen the same story I'd told Mr. Bowles. But I could see that Mr. Shen wasn't satisfied with my answer, but he made out as though he was.

"Vacation is a good idea," he said. "Doc said you lost your mother. Sometimes then a fellow should take time out to kind of catch his breath. Then again, maybe he shouldn't. Maybe he should keep busy."

All of a sudden I had the urge to blurt out the whole story. I wanted someone to know. I had been carrying the thing around inside me for so long that it seemed if I didn't talk to someone about it, I was just going to bust wide open. I wanted to lean across the desk and say: "Mr. Shen, I'm in real trouble. My dad is awful sick and I don't know what to do any more. I can't take care of him, and instead of getting better he's getting worse. I'm afraid he might be thinking of doing away with himself. I need help, Mr. Shen. I need help real bad."

Something of what I was thinking must have showed on my face, because Mr. Shen leaned forward and said, "Yes? Was there something?"

Right then and there I probably could have thrown down my load and let someone else pick it up. The temptation to ask for help almost overwhelmed me.

But I couldn't do it. Not yet. I hadn't played my hand out. I still held a few cards. There was the big snake. Ironheaded or not, when we came to town I wanted it our way. I didn't want to come with my hand out begging.

So I braced a little in the chair, and when I felt the tears start coming in back of my eyes, I blinked so they wouldn't show and I said, "Well, we aren't exactly loafing, Mr. Shen. We keep pretty busy. There's always the snakes, and Dad never gets his fill of fishing, so he goes to the river almost every day, and it's getting so he throws back more fish than we eat."

I thought that last might throw him off the trail a little, and maybe it did, because he was smiling easy now and he said, "Fine. Fine, Doug. You know you're one of my best snake men. You always bring me good snakes. But good snakes or not, we Crackers have got to stick together. So if there ever is anything I can do for you, don't be bashful about asking. I mean it now, Doug. You come right in, and if I can help I will."

I tried a smile and maybe it came off, and then I got up and said, "That's nice of you, Mr. Shen, and I'll remember it."

Then I said good-bye to Mr. Shen and Mr. Bowles, because I wanted to get out of there. I felt like running, but I made myself put one foot slowly right down in front of the other. Then when I got through the door the tears that had been forming up in back of my eyes put a little film forward so that it was a little hard to see, and I bumped right into one of the office girls and she gasped. Out of the corner of my eye then, I got just a glimpse of Mr. Bowles and Mr. Shen, and they were both watching me through the big window in the office. So I hurried a little to get outside.

Well, where was my luck now? I thought, as I hit the hot street. The day had started out to be too good to last. A half-hour ago I felt like things were going right down my alley, and now I didn't know. I had a feeling that maybe I hadn't seen or heard the last of Doc Bellamy and Mr. Shen. It was pretty plain that they suspected something was wrong.

I walked downtown to Hyacinth City to get groceries and then went over to the bus depot. On the way home I sat right behind the driver since it was someone I'd never seen before and I'd have to tell him where to stop to let me off.

One thing was for sure now. Doc Bellamy was on my trail because he didn't believe my story about living near Immokalee. It was certain too, that if he and Mr.

94

Shen ever compared stories they'd both know I was lying. If Mr. Bowles hadn't been sitting there I might have been able to find some way around telling Mr. Shen where we lived. But Mr. Bowles knew, so how could I?

Well, now I had to find that snake and find it fast. With five hundred dollars I didn't care what they found out, because we wouldn't be welfare cases.

Maybe five hundred wouldn't last long, but it would be a start, and by the time it was used up I'd be working steady for sure somewhere, and then I'd be able to make weekly payments.

Perhaps I could even get a job with Mr. Shen, because I was handy with snakes. I could milk them for venom, and I could do a good job of skinning so the skins would be in nice shape.

My mind galloped along like that and I missed my stop; by the time the bus pulled over I had a little piece to walk back under that hot sun, and with the heat coming out of the ground as fiercely as it was coming out of the sky.

It was a relief to be able to turn into the trail and have the trees overhead, and after walking awhile I sat down to rest and to see if I could get my thinking straightened out and make some plans.

But the more I tried to plan, the more I couldn't. So I was right back where I'd started, and that meant taking each day as it came along and doing what had to be done, and then letting the day after that take care of itself when I came to it.

So tomorrow I'd hunt for the snake, and every day

after that unless something came along to interrupt my plans.

I moved more slowly now because the heat had finally tired me. The dust was coming all the way up to my knees every time I put a boot to the trail. The scrub was gray with dust, and the sinkholes were getting cracks wide enough to fall into.

A rain would sure be wonderful, I thought. Sometimes when it got this hot the big, black clouds boiled right up out of nowhere. They came so fast even an airplane had trouble staying out ahead of them. They were so thick then, that it got dark as evening, and when the rain came it didn't fall in drops, but swept down hard in solid sheets.

But it didn't rain, and when I got back to the shack there wasn't a cloud anywhere, and it was only a little less hot because I was in the shade of the Piny Woods and the sun was hanging low to the horizon.

I unlocked the padlock, and Dad looked up when I opened the door. "Come on out, Dad," I said. "Come on out to the log." He was wet with sweat, and he got up without me going to him and came out to sit on the log. But it was no better outside than it had been inside.

I put a piece of side pork in a kettle and began boiling it, and I opened a can of beans and, for a special treat, I put a bottle of catchup on the table. Then I remembered the trout. Well, this heat had probably spoiled them anyway, so I took them out of the butter hole and threw them away.

The pork was done by the time it was dark, and it

was a little cooler though still sticky, and as we ate in the lamplight, I said to Dad: "It won't be long now, Dad, and something is bound to happen. One way or another, things are going to change. I'm sure of it, Dad."

This was the feeling that had come over me, and I knew that it was finally true, that in one way or another things were going to change. I didn't know if it was going to be for better or worse. But I knew it wouldn't be long one way or another. And though I didn't feel good about it, I didn't feel bad either. I was just glad to think that a change was coming, and with that on my mind, I slept well.

CHAPTER 9

❧ The heat was still a solid thing in the morning. There were no birds left to hover over Cypress Pond, so I knew that by now it was a graveyard of bleached bones. Only some turtles would live. A few would move overland to other water holes, and a few others would dig down into the mud and wait for rains to put water back into the hole.

Some insects would burrow into the mud, and a few minnows might survive for a while. Some minnows were tough enough to live on a wet leaf, and they'd hang on somehow if it wasn't too long between rains. Some day, of course, Cypress Pond might fill up again. The hole where it drained away might become plugged with silt, or an underground river would break through the crust somewhere, and then it would be alive again.

But right now it was dead, and there wasn't a rain

cloud anywhere. I could almost see the grass underfoot turn brown. If this kept up the sinkhole where we got our water would dry up, and I'd have to go hunting around for another. So right after breakfast I filled all the cans and even the kettles. I'd boil the whole lot tonight so we wouldn't run out of drinking water for a while.

It surely was no day to go hunting for the big snake. No snake with even a speck of a brain would risk as much as two minutes in this sun. It'd stay in the cooler tunnels and caves underground, or next to damp logs or in the thick scrub where no slice of sun could squeeze through.

Not even a frog would be able to survive the direct sunlight on a day like this. It would shrivel right up as the sun soaked up its juices and there, instead of a frog, would be a frog skin. I'd seen it happen. Sun could soak the life right out of cold-blooded creatures, evaporate life right into the air like it was water.

But I was going snake hunting anyway. Maybe I'd find some sign, its track in the sand—anything—a cast-off skin to give me hope that the snake was still alive.

Locking Dad in the shack today would be an act of mercy. If he stayed out in the sun he'd roast alive. When I touched the lock to snap it, the metal burned my hand.

I left the clearing slowly. Usually I started my day at a half trot. But today I deliberately dragged my feet.

When I came to the trail that turned down to where I'd had the snake by the tail, I leaned against a tree and rested awhile. The sky was like a white-hot sheet of metal. There wasn't a bird up there, not even any buzzards flying patrol. Today the birds would sit in the thick cover with their beaks open and they'd pant like dogs to keep cool. They'd ruffle their feathers against the heat the same way they ruffled them against the cold.

While I leaned there I wondered if Mr. Shen would call Doc Bellamy at Evenset and tell him that Dad and I were living somewhere in Big Swampy. I wondered if Doc had said: "If you find out where they're living, give me a call collect and let me know."

Doc would be like that. He'd been the Evenset doctor since before Dad was born. I doubt that there were many persons in Evenset under forty that he hadn't brought into the world. You'd think he owned the town, that he was everybody's father, and in some ways I guess that was right.

I couldn't think of anybody in Evenset who had as much right to the lives of the people as Doc Bellamy had. He slapped them alive and he closed their eyes when they died, and he just kept going on and on.

I liked Doc Bellamy, and there's nothing I'd rather have than him on my side. But what could he do when the chips were all in? What could he do with Dad? Sit with him? Nurse him? No, he'd have to send him away, and that would be an end to that.

I thought about yesterday. How could it start out so lucky? I was sure things were going to work out. Luck runs like that, in streaks. But my luck had run out just as it was getting up a good head of steam. I sure didn't feel lucky today.

I shrugged myself out of it, and using the forked stick to lean on, started down the path. Birds let me pass without jumping into the air. Even the timid scrub jays just sat and looked at me. There weren't even any flies buzzing.

When I came to the shriveled palmetto frond that I'd cut to mark the place where I'd had the snake by the tail, I knelt to smell in the hole. There had been no snake in there recently, of that I was sure.

I began my careful circling maneuver again, paying special attention to the open sandy areas where a crawling snake might lay a track. There were many bird tracks and some animal tracks, but I saw no snake trails.

My circles kept widening until I was skirting a sandy rift on one side and dropping lower toward the river on the other.

Then, just as I was about to give up, I found a trail, and it was broad enough across and deep enough in the sand to have been made by but one snake—the big one!

The snake was alive! I hadn't killed it that day I hung to its tail.

I found the trail in a clearing about six feet across. The grass had shriveled to dust, but the snake trail was unmistakable—a winding, slithering slide through the sand all the way across to where the scrub started. It was hard to tell the snake's direction, but I thought it was headed north.

I broke a frond of palmetto so that it drooped and marked the spot—if I had to I could come back to it.

Then I began the difficult task of tracking. It wasn't really tracking in the sense of following the trail. That would have been impossible. The snake's body had left no imprint on hard ground or where it had slithered through the scrub. Only where it crossed sandy clearings did I see the shallow groove.

But by working a circle and studying each little clearing, I was able to determine the snake's general direction, and it appeared to me that it was headed for Mirror River.

There was no way of telling how old the sign was. In some places birds and animals had walked in the trail, and where wind had fingered down through the scrub, it had filled the depression with sand until it was barely visible. But I was making good progress, nevertheless, because once I had determined what I thought the snake's direction was, I could always mark the last place where it had left a sign and then travel forward until I found other evidence of its passing.

I was becoming certain also that I was traveling in the right direction and not backtracking the snake. The farther I got along, the easier the trail became to follow. Sometimes it disappeared beneath tree roots, and then didn't appear again until forty or fifty feet farther along. Once it ended in a burrow, and I thought the snake had gone below to hunt out some furred animal or take refuge from the sun.

By noon the heat had exhausted me. I had never wanted water so badly. Lying in the shade of a palmetto to rest, I tried wetting my dry lips with my tongue, but there was no saliva for them. My eyes burned and felt rough, as though I had gotten sand into them. Heat records for Florida were certainly being broken today, I thought. Well, when I got to the river I'd lie in the water and let my body soak it up.

But I was still a long way from the river, and if the snake sign continued in the same direction, I would have to cross a great flat swamp without a tree or bush on it to shade me from the sun. In wet times I wouldn't have dared to cross the treacherous pocket, but I felt sure that, considering the weather we'd been having, it would be safe.

As the scrub diminished, the trail of the snake became easier to follow. There was no doubt that it would cross the swamp; the snake had probably been headed for the rise that marked the banks of the Mirror River. The high ground along the river was good snake country. There were rock crevices, and a dense growth of practically every grass, bush, and tree native to central Florida.

There was an abundance of food for snakes, and I had taken many kinds along the river bank, including a few water moccasins, what we called cottonmouths, and some copperheads. They were too unpredictable, and they never gave a warning like a rattler. But when I came across one, I'd slip it into the bag and Mr. Shen would give me a few dollars for it, and add it to his exhibits.

When I broke clear of the scrub and started across the swamp, the sun slammed me. I could feel my skin shrivel, and I hunted hard for a snake sign so I could get across and into the shade along the river bank.

At intervals I found the trail, and it led straight across, so I thought to hurry in that direction, hoping to be able to discover where on the other side the snake had gone into the cover.

Of course, I should have known better than to hurry in a swamp. Dry or wet, they are treacherous places. What's worse is that the dangerous places do not look dangerous. The seemingly solid ground can suddenly open up.

But I was suffering from the sun, and in my eagerness to get into the shade and then take off my clothes and lie in the cool river, I hurried straight across the heat-caked muck holes, leaving muddy tracks even where the sun had opened great cracks in the earth.

I didn't get halfway across, and was hurrying over a wide, sun-cracked sinkhole when the ground suddenly opened up and I sank waist-deep into a mess of marl.

I panicked for a few seconds and struggled frantically. During those few seconds I managed to sink myself another foot into the white slop, and then it held me tight as a vise.

Marl is worse than quicksand. It presses in on a victim with painful pressure from all sides. Depending on how much water the stuff contains, it can hold a cow or open up to swallow a coon. Sometimes it is only a few feet deep, but I'd found places where a twenty-foot pole wouldn't hit bottom.

I bent far forward, hoping to lever my feet up and by pulling forward with my hands, get the weight of my body out flat. But my feet wouldn't budge, and I only managed to make claw marks in the sinkhole crust.

One thing, though, if I was sinking deeper, it was very slowly. There had to be a way, and I tried to think, but the hot sun on my head seemed to be frying my brains. It was almost unbearable.

Once more I struggled to free myself. There was a tuft of saw grass maybe six feet beyond the reach of my hands. If I could only get hold of it. Leaning forward, I stretched as if by some miracle my body would become elastic and I might get a grip on it.

But my struggles only put me in deeper and tighter, and stirring up the marl made it stink like things long dead. The stench made me sick to my stomach. It was the odor of hundreds, maybe thousands of years of rotting Everglades life.

Now I wondered if I was doomed to become a part of that marl hole and in the end a part of the Everglades, of Big Swampy.

The thought made me frantic and again I tried to throw myself forward and lever my feet back to the surface. But it wasn't working. Already the marl was up to my shirt pocket.

I tried to turn, but only managed to swing my head so I could look behind me. There was a small log, but it too was beyond my reach.

My strength was going. I could feel it. If the sun hadn't been a blazing furnace breathing all its heat down onto me, there might have been a chance. But now I wondered how long I'd last. Would I make it until nighttime? Maybe I would. Maybe I would. Then when it cooled, I might find some way. I had to last. I was tough, like a bull-leather boot lace. I'd hang on.

So I relaxed a little, and when I did it hit me. Dad was back in the shack! Locked in! It shook me so, I started shouting for help even though I knew there was no one to hear except the birds.

"Dear Lord," I heard myself saying, "don't let it happen!"

If I died it would be quick compared to the way he'd go. When the food and water gave out, he'd. . . .

What a fool I'd been to lock him up! It was like murdering him.

Then the first fear for him having run through me, I felt strangely quiet inside. So, this was the way all of it, everything, was going to end. In trying to save him, I was killing him and myself. This was really the bottom of the pit, and we were both in it.

I could feel tears in my eyes, and I heard a sob come out of my lungs, only it didn't sound like I had sobbed, but as though the whole earth below me had sobbed.

When the sobbing passed, I tried to get hold of myself. Again I spread my arms like a bird its wings, and though I knew it was useless. I tried to lift.

Time seemed to gradually fade away then. I think maybe I lost consciousness—at least a little—because I had some weird dreams about sitting on a cloud and eating oranges. I haven't any idea how much time passed, but all of a sudden my senses seemed to come back into sharp focus, and I could see a fly crawling on a grass stem twenty feet away, and I could smell the river though it was too far away to smell, and I heard a heat bug far back in the bush and it sounded so close it seemed I ought to be able to see it.

Maybe this was all part of dying. I could even taste water, and the marl instead of clutching and pressing in on me seemed to hold me soft and warm like a fuzzy blanket.

God, I thought, what is happening? Is this the way it ends?

And then, as part of the same dream or whatever it was, I saw smoke clouds rising in the sky, and I thought: "Someone has set fire to Big Swampy." Then I wondered if maybe the fire would get me first.

I tried to tell myself I was imagining it all, but it was no good, and I saw smoke clouds rising in the sky and flames shooting through them. It was all moving swiftly, like a fire does, straight toward me.

Then I felt the first breeze of fire on my face, but instead of scorching me, it cooled me, and then I knew I was out of my mind, that I was imagining all these things.

The smoke clouds were over me now, and I still hadn't been burned by the fire, and I imagined that a drop of water had touched my face. Then another, and another. . . .

So, this is how it was. Not hard at all. Easy to go.

I put a finger to my cheek, and even my finger could feel the water. I put the wet finger to my dry lips, and they tasted the water.

It *was* water!

I raised my eyes to the smoke above me where white

fire was flashing and the roar of flames was a persistent rumbling . . . and then I knew quite suddenly that it wasn't smoke. I knew then they were great, black thunderclouds, and the fire I had seen was lightning flashing.

I felt more drops of water on my face. Then it seemed the sky opened up and the rain came in such a deluge I had to close my eyes to the force of it.

Never, never, never had I felt anything so wonderfully refreshing. It was like the coolness of ice. It was like the softness of cream. It poured through my brittle hair. It soothed the soreness of my eyes. It touched my dry lips like a kiss.

I was alive, and I told myself I *would* live, and that I'd get out of that sinkhole, and I'd go back to the shack and unlock the door so Dad could come out and sit on the log and soak up the rain.

Within minutes there were several inches of water on the sinkhole crust, and the cracks closed as though by magic, and the dark surface turned to a creamy, silvery white as it turned liquid. I stirred it with my hands and arms until the top layer was like water.

I shifted the upper part of my body, and it moved back and forth. The rain continued to fall in solid sheets. I couldn't see the saw grass ten feet away. Great volumes of water fell as though a lake had been dropped out of the sky and was hitting the earth with a tremendous splash.

I kept working my arms and my body, stirring the marl until I had a foot or more on top thin enough to swim in.

I guess I shouted with joy, but then I made myself keep silent and concentrate on loosening the marl around my body. Deeper and deeper my hands and arms went as I made one huge mixing bowl out of the sinkhole.

I could feel the pressure ease off my waist and then my thighs. When the water got as low as my feet, I was either going to sink out of sight or swim out of that mess.

Then I felt a foot loosen. I did what I knew I had to do. With a quick and gigantic effort I threw myself forward, straight and flat, and began swimming for my life. I did the breast stroke and kicked with all the strength I had.

At first I didn't move, but I didn't sink either. I kept pumping my legs up and down, and as the marl became more watery I increased the speed of the kick. I kept raising myself into the air with the breast stroke. Then I went forward a few inches. I could feel my feet break out into the air. I was swimming, and now there was no stopping or I'd go straight down and that surely would be the end.

I took a deep breath and held it. It buoyed me up. I expelled the air and quickly filled my lungs again. Then when I felt myself lifting higher and higher, I did the crawl and began to swim through the slime to where I could get my hands on a bunch of saw grass. With all my strength I pulled and kicked until I came out of the slime like some frantic lizard.

I dragged myself until only my feet were in the sinkhole, and then I lay still, letting the rain beat on me, letting the water wash me, letting life come slowly back into my bones.

I had made it. I knew I had made it. Now there was no need except to lay there tasting the air in my throat and feeling it fill my lungs and being cool and wet, and putting my sore tongue to the wetness of my lips, and waiting for strength so I could crawl farther and farther from the sinkhole to where the earth was solid, solid, solid.

At last I could raise my arms and it was like a prayer. I held them up toward the sky I couldn't see, and was almost frantically grateful.

Then I began crawling slowly until I hit a high piece of ground, and here I sat and watched the rain wash the last of the slime off my boots and saw the silvery marl run away from my pants' legs through the saw grass, and watched the sinkhole fill with water.

The rain beat down on me for another ten minutes, and then the boiling, angry, black clouds passed on and the dim day brightened and, just as swiftly as it had come, the shower ended. The sun shone and it was a hot sun, but now there was a breeze. My wet clothes were plastered to my body, and I felt that I would like to stay wet the rest of my life and always have the breeze blowing on me.

I got up slowly, and threading my way carefully between the sinkholes, which were now filled with water, I went back to the freshly washed scrub. Now the birds were alert to my passing, and every palm and palmetto and every bush and tree had turned from dusty gray to brilliant green.

I had never thought that just being alive could be so excitingly important. All the trouble that had been driving me nearly out of my mind lost a lot of its significance. Compared to my resurrection, the big snake's capture seemed only a little detail to be taken care of when that time came. There were *no* problems for me now that couldn't be solved. I'd find some way to solve them—all of them, every one.

If I could be alive again and be here walking with the wind on my face and the world washed clean and the birds singing and the flies buzzing—then there wasn't a thing I couldn't do—nothing, nothing, nothing.

CHAPTER 10

❧ The good, strong feeling didn't leave me. Not when I unlocked the shack door and brought Dad out onto the log, not while I ate supper, not when the stars came out.

"Maybe," I thought, "I have learned something." By getting out of that sinkhole, all the other things in my life had been put back where they belonged, into their proper places. Now none of them seemed impossible.

I felt I could do anything, that I could see my way through, and that I wasn't going to give up and go crying to Doc Bellamy and Mr. Shen for help. It seemed like I was big enough and strong enough to do what had to be done by myself.

Yesterday, the day before . . . I guess I would have been happy to have had Doc walk into the shack clearing and say: "Okay, Doug. You've had your chance. Now I'm taking over. From here on out your worries are over." But not today, not tonight. Now I was sure the big snake was along the river bank somewhere, and now I was sure that I could find him.

And once I found that snake and delivered it to the Reptile Institute, the other things would start falling into place. I had so much faith in myself that I knew I couldn't fail. It was almost as though I'd had a vision, that I'd seen how everything would work out if only I didn't lose heart.

In some ways it was as though I'd been made over. It seemed the old, weak, doubting parts of me had been thrown away and new and stronger parts had replaced them. Maybe that's what people meant when they talked about "being born again."

Whatever it was, it sure was a good feeling. I only hoped it would stay with me. I only hoped that when the going got rough I could remember the feeling, and know deep down that there always is a way. I hoped it would give me the strength to get things rolling on the right track so I could lead Dad down that trail, out onto the road where we could wave the bus down . . . and then have Doc get Dad and take him to the hospital while I looked for work in Hyacinth City.

I went to sleep with the good, strong feeling, and if it was less strong next morning, on being faced with another day, it was still there, and I got myself and Dad ready so I could hike myself right to that river bank and start looking for the big snake.

I could even sing while making breakfast, and I thought part of the reason might be because Big Swampy was so washed and clean. The dust had been laid. The sky was fresh and clean. The odor of pine pitch, strong as turpentine, was in the air, and when the smoke came out of the shack chimney, it didn't rise a little way only to flatten out and come down again, but the breeze caught and carried it in gray threads among the pine needles.

There were even some birds hovering over Cypress Pond, so I assumed the rain had put some water into it and brought the insects and minnows—maybe even some fish—back up out of the bottom.

It was amazing how rain could make things come to life. In a day grass that had been matted down was standing straight and there were slivers of new green starting right out of the sand. Bushes, their leaves so wilted they looked dead, had taken to growing and glowing. Even the sand gleamed in the sun as though it had been scrubbed.

I fried some ham for a treat to go with the grits, and I drank three scalding cups of coffee, and then I sat awhile, glad to just look and breathe. Then I locked Dad up, got my sacks and the forked stick, and started down the trail.

While I walked I wondered how it was that I could feel so strong and alive today when yesterday I had been as close to death as a few minutes. How could a man want to die one minute and then suddenly want to live more than anything else in the world? Could Dad feel that, a sudden change like that? Could he too come quickly alive? I wondered.

Water still stood in the deep shade like diamonds on

the leaves. Lizards ran off the sunny path to hide where the sun couldn't come to them. Today the scrub jays jumped when I came down the trail and went off telling about how I was trespassing on their territory. Today there were some redbirds whistling sharp and clear, and the buzzards were flying their silent, watchful patrols and not missing even a leaf that had been turned over during the night.

There were little marsh wrens flitting along the edge where saw grass and cattails blended, and above there was a procession of little and large terns, cranes, herons, ducks, and even pelicans flying their solemn formation to some inland adventure.

It was surprising how on one day a pond could be dry and deserted, and after a downpour become suddenly inhabited by limpkins and gallinules, ducks and coots, and scores of little water chickens running from one bit of floating vegetation to another almost as though they were walking on water.

Where did they come from? Out of the sky? Hatched by the thunder? One instant there were none, and then but turn your head and the potholes were nervous with their movements and sounds.

I moved swiftly though quietly along, because I wanted all the hours of daylight to search for the snake. I would do it methodically. I would start at a place on the ridge of high ground and go over it carefully, back and forth all along the river. If the snake was there, and I felt sure that it was, I wasn't going to walk past it. I'd pry into every hole and crevice, look under every root and rock. I'd move from the water across the small ridge to the swamp and back to the water again, leaving not even a leaf unturned.

I stayed off the dim trail that led to the flats where I had blundered into the sinkhole. Instead I followed the beaten path toward the road, intending to take a right-angle turn at a point where it came near the river.

I walked half a mile on the trail, and then I swung north through some thick scrub to hit out into grass-lands filled with innumerable green islands of palm and palmetto. I hurried without looking for a snake-sign, and was almost beyond hearing range of the main trail when something stopped me.

I was sure I'd heard voices. I dropped to my knees and was quiet, but there was nothing, only the rustle of a palm on a nearby hammock and a dove mourning and the questions some terns were asking back and forth about the fishing.

I couldn't have been mistaken. There is no mistaking the sound of the human voice—not in Big Swampy where the human voice is seldom heard.

But who? A hopeful pig hunter? A game protector? Another snake hunter who somehow had blundered across the big one? A poacher? But none of these would likely talk, not loud enough for me to hear. They'd come quietly because they were here about a business that asks for quiet.

I took a few steps to where I could hide in taller grass and settled to a comfortable position to wait. Some tiny song birds flitted in close around. Even a scrub jay forgot that I was walking across its country and sat on a limb close enough to have been stoned.

Then I heard it again. I had not been mistaken. There were voices on the trail I'd just left.

Crouching low, I moved from hammock to hammock until I was back in the scrub, and then I crawled carefully to a point from which I could see anyone using the trail.

Now I could hear sticks breaking underfoot and branches being pushed aside and flipping back again. Whoever it was, they were not trying to conceal their presence, nor were they hunting for anything. They were blundering along like cows.

Then I heard a voice that lifted the little hairs on my arms with apprehension. It was Doc Bellamy's voice.

"Wonder how far in they are?" he was asking.

"Don't imagine it is too far. Bowles said the boy was out on the road by noon, and that was after hunting awhile." The other voice was that of Mr. Shen.

Then both men came into view, disappeared behind some brush, and then were visible again. Mr. Shen in high snake boots and using a professional snake stick as a staff, was leading the way. He was moving slowly, probably so Doc would have no difficulty keeping up.

Now there couldn't be any doubt. Doc had not believed my story. He was convinced something was wrong, and he was coming to find out.

I might have known I couldn't fool Doc. I wondered if anybody ever had.

I flattened out as they approached and breathed as

softly as I could. They passed within twenty feet and disappeared in the scrub.

I let them get down the trail aways, and then I got up and, moving as swiftly as I could through the undergrowth and around the sinkholes, I cut out in a wide circle.

If I moved fast enough maybe I could beat them. At any rate, I was going to try. Today I wanted to do things my way. Two days ago I would have welcomed them, because two days ago I had been beaten.

But I wasn't beaten now, and I wasn't going to give up until I had to. Maybe going to the hospital might not even cure Dad. Doc had never said it was a *sure* cure. He had talked about how in the end Dad would probably have to cure himself. I could still remember his words:

"The hospital would be the place for him," he'd said. "They could help, more than anywhere else. But it would be up to the Duke too. He'd have to try, to want to cure himself—unless something suddenly shocked him to his senses."

So why should he go in now when we didn't have a dime? I didn't see how I could. Maybe I was an ironhead like Dad used to say. Well, ironhead or not, I was too close now, too close to getting enough to help ourselves. At least we could be independent.

I admired Doc, but I couldn't let that matter.

What surprised me most was that Mr. Shen thought enough of me to go to the trouble of bringing Doc to Big Swampy.

But I couldn't quit! Not today! Not with the good strong feeling I had. If I quit now, whatever way I looked at it, I wouldn't be giving Dad the chance I had planned. The snake was out there somewhere. Big snakes don't just evaporate. That meant five hundred dollars. With five hundred dollars I could at least call the turn.

I loped through the scrub and at times the thorny bushes grabbed at me and at times a branch slapped me in the face. But I kept a steady pace, and then when I thought I was far out ahead, I turned and started toward the shack.

When I came to the dim path on which I'd walked to the flat full of sinkholes, I turned onto it, and here I could make better time because deer had been using it and keeping it fairly clear.

Where the dim path met the road path down which the two men were coming, I stopped to listen. I could hear nothing, so I turned and started running again, and in a moment could see the shack.

I stopped running in the clearing and walked the rest of the way to catch my breath. Then I put the key in the lock and snapped it open. Dad was seated at the table looking out a window.

"Come on, Dad," I said, "we're going for a walk."

I went over and took his arm and he got up. I knew I couldn't run with him, so I took the path to Piny Woods where the arrow of trees pointed to Cypress Pond. After we were a little way from the shack, I dropped Dad's arm, and he followed along behind.

When I got to the stump where I'd always sat, I stood and looked back and listened. Still no sound, nor was there anyone in sight. If they came up while I was crossing the clearing they would see me, but I had to chance it.

"Come on, Dad," I said, and started off into the knee-high saw grass.

Dad followed and when we got to the trees that surrounded the pond, I knew we had made it—at least for now. We went through the trees all the way to the mucky ground, and then I went to my knees beneath a cypress tree and pulled Dad down alongside me.

It wasn't long before I heard voices. Leaving Dad, I crawled on my hands and knees to the edge of the cover. Looking out across the clearing, I could get brief glimpses of the two men moving about through the clearing, and though I could hear them, I couldn't make out what they were saying.

I crawled back to make sure Dad was all right, and then I crawled back to the edge again. They must have gone into the shack, because I could neither hear nor see them. They'd probably settle down to wait, hoping we'd come back. It would be a long, wasted day.

But tomorrow would be another day, and I had a feeling that snake wasn't going anywhere. At least, I hoped it wasn't. I hoped it would like its new grounds well enough to stay there until I removed it.

A little smoke from the chimney told me they were making coffee or perhaps something to eat. I hoped Mr. Shen wouldn't decide to hunt snakes while he was in Big Swampy and wander toward Cypress Pond. If he got too close, he might spot our tracks in the muck at the edge of the clearing. Mr. Shen would know they were fresh. He'd be on our trail in a second, and have us in the next. He'd been born and raised in this kind of country, and could track a caterpillar across a swept sidewalk.

There was nothing Mr. Shen did not know about the Glades. I'd listened when he'd been out working around the snakes, and he could tell by touch which snake was going to die before sundown. He could tell by the way a bird flew if its crop was full or empty, if the bird was coming from or going to a nest, whether it was hunting food or merely sightseeing. If Mr. Shen had any idea we were close about, he'd hunt us out, and there'd be nothing I could do to hide the trail.

I crawled back and sprawled out beside Dad. He had put his head back against the trunk of the tree and was resting. I lay on my stomach and put my chin in my cupped hands. There were sounds about, but they seemed distant under the covering of trees. Even the birds we had sent winging when we first came into the tree fringe had settled back down before Doc and Mr. Shen had arrived at the cabin.

If Mr. Shen had seen the birds circling, he might have guessed someone was at the pond, but maybe not. Sometimes a bobcat could spook birds, and they would hang in the air scolding until the cat went away.

It was a sleepy way to spend the day, lying there with only a little sun filtering through to make patches of brightness on the ground. I would have liked to spend many days like this, resting under a cypress, looking at the sun spots on the leaves and how they changed shape as the sun moved across the sky. And maybe someday I'd be able to.

Then I heard voices again, so I crawled back to the edge and looked out. Both men were in the clearing, and then it looked like one of them sat on Dad's log and the other started off toward the Piny Woods.

If I guessed right, Doc was going to sit and rest while Mr. Shen did some scouting. I had known he would. Mr. Shen wasn't the sort of person to sit in camp and wait for people who lived there to come back. He'd have to nose around a little.

At least there was no chance he could trail us in Piny Woods. The ground was too hard, and the pine needles didn't take a boot print, but bounced right back. The only danger of discovery would come if he got too close to the spot where we'd entered the rim of Cypress Pond trees.

From time to time I could get glimpses of him moving among the pines. Once he stopped, and I was sure it was where I killed the boar. There was nothing but scattered white bones there now, since the birds and the animals had cleaned up the meat, but Mr. Shen would have known Dad or I killed the animal. He'd be able to read the sign and see the bullet hole in the skull.

He didn't stay at the patch of scrub long, but moved on down the path, and then he broke out of the trees alongside the stump where I'd always sat. He'd know the stump was a favorite sitting place. It was well worn from sliding on and off it.

Where he was standing his back was to me, and I hoped it would stay that way. He was scanning the wide, open grass country, and I knew his eyes were traveling from hammock to hammock looking for some sign. I wondered if we'd kicked up enough mud where we'd entered the trees so it was visible from where he was standing. I hoped not.

He turned slowly, and finally he was facing Cypress Pond. I froze, though I knew he couldn't see us.

Then he started in our direction, but stopped. He stood for a long time looking directly at the spot where we were hiding. I was thankful the birds weren't circling. If they had he surely would have walked across the clearing to investigate.

Once again he started walking toward the pond, but he took only a few steps. He put his hands over his eyes to shade them from the sun. Then slowly he turned away and began scanning the flat grass country again.

He was taking his time about it so he wouldn't miss a thing. Finally he walked over to the stump and sat down.

Perhaps he was satisfied that we hadn't crossed the clearing, or perhaps he still wasn't convinced that we weren't out there somewhere and thought to wait around.

His head was turned away from Cypress Pond now, and I felt better about that. I just was beginning to relax when I heard a sound behind me, and swinging about saw Dad coming toward me through the trees. I ran back and pulled him to the ground. The sound sent a rash of terns screaming, and I could see Mr. Shen's head whip around to watch the birds.

I lay holding Dad to the ground, waiting for Mr. Shen to come. He got down off the stump and started toward the pond. Then when no other birds followed the terns into the air, he went back and sat down again.

The terns settled quickly back to the pond surface where they'd been flying leisurely patrol, and I figured Mr. Shen was writing off their complaint to the presence of some predator bird or animal.

He sat for another fifteen or twenty minutes, and then, seemingly satisfied, he got down from the stump and headed back toward the shack. When he was among the trees, I led Dad back to where he'd been lying under the cypress.

"Dad, you've just got to stay here," I said.

Then I leaned back beside him and waited. It wasn't long before I heard voices again. I crawled back to the edge of the clearing and lay watching. Doc had gotten up off the log, and I could see they were standing and talking.

Then they both went inside the shack, and everything was quiet, so I supposed they might be having a siesta while they waited. I dozed a few times, but I kept fearing Dad might move again and send the birds into the air.

The sun topped out and started silding down the sky, and I'm sure I must have fallen asleep because next thing I knew the shadows of the pines across the clearing were lying out flat and long, straight toward me.

Voices had awakened me, and I could see Doc and Mr. Shen were out in the clearing again. If they didn't leave now, they'd never get out of Big Swampy before dark, and I didn't think that Mr. Shen would like to have Doc with him in the scrub after the sun was down.

I was right. They were leaving. I got a glimpse as they swung off and around the outhouse to hit the trail. For a few seconds I could hear their voices, and then it was quiet.

I gave them plenty of time, and then went back to get Dad. He was sleeping, so I woke him and, taking him by the arm, walked out into the clearing. I stood there for a few minutes, but when there was no sign of the two men, I crossed over with Dad following and went into the shack.

On the table was bread, butter, some cans of beans, and a big chunk of cheese. There was also a note. It read:

"Dear Duke: Heard you were baching it out here in Big Swampy, so thought I'd drop in to say hello. Sorry I didn't catch you at home. Here's a few things we had left over from lunch. When you get to town, drop in to see me." It was signed: "Doc".

So Doc was playing it smooth. He wasn't going to let on that he thought we were in trouble. Doc could be awfully polite about not seeing things, whether it was death in a patient's eyes, a leg so shattered it had to come off, or maybe just a housewife who still had her hair in curlers when Doc came making a call.

He'd be back, that was for sure. Either that or he'd make some arrangement with Mr. Shen to keep me around when I brought in a snake so he could get a chance to talk to me. Doc didn't just give up.

CHAPTER 11

The next morning a kingfisher flashed like a blue arrow to announce my arrival at Mirror River, and with a war cry it rattled up and back along the slick of brown water, telling all other forms of life that an intruder was along the bank.

I'd gotten up long before dawn, and having fed Dad and locked him in, started down the trail even before the east had shown any signs of splintering the night.

I had no fear of visitors this day. If they were going to come back, they'd wait awhile first. There'd be work for both to make up for the day they had missed.

I had traveled fast, and the sun was like a big eye on the horizon, getting its first look at today's world, so I thought I'd rest for a few minutes before starting my search.

There were some fish crows down on a bend where a mud flat showed, and I thought maybe they had found

127

a dead trout washed ashore. The undergrowth sparkled with many kinds of little birds, most of which I didn't have names for.

The brown water of the river moved like syrup, and from time to time it broke into rings when fish surfaced. It would have been fun just to spend the day soaking a gator flea for bream, or dangling a piece of pork back among the hyacinths for trout, or soaking a piece of gut for the catfish that cruised the bottoms of the deep holes.

How many days ago was it that I promised myself I'd take a day off and go fishing? Less than a week? Well, it seemed like a year, like a hundred years. In a whole lifetime not as much had happened to me as had happened during the past week. It didn't seem possible that so much could be crowded into such a short time. But there it was—day after day, night after night—and no denying it.

But my day would come. I believed that. And when it came, I knew Dad would be beside me leaning back against the trunk of a tree and drinking a can of beer and telling stories while I tended the lines.

The morning, cool almost to being crisp, had put a little mist in the back bays, but the sun was getting in a lick or two. It came through the whiteness of the mist in thick rays like it comes through church windows. It was almost too beautiful to miss by moving. So I sat a little while longer, because it seemed the air hadn't warmed enough to bring the snakes up and out, and I didn't want to miss the big one by walking past a place where it had denned.

If a man put a boat in the river here and let it drift, it would ride him all the way to Diamond Springs. There the stream got a big, fresh supply of water and, making a hairpin turn, went back toward the Atlantic Ocean. I'd floated it to Diamond Springs—Dad and I had. But we'd never made the trip to the Ocean. Maybe someday we would.

But first the snake—so I got up and started carefully poking through the brush. I covered the ground as I had planned, moving to the swamp on the one side, and then crossing the bank and over to the river on the other. Back and forth.

I used the snake stick as a finder, poking it into every bit of brush, turning stones with it, and rolling over sticks and prying under logs. If someone had lost a dime on the river bank, I was going to find it. And if that big snake was there, he was as good as in the bag right now.

The mist from the back bays didn't get very high. The sun burned if off before it had reached the lowest limbs of the big cypress. I could feel its warmth through my shirt, so I knew it was going to be a good snake-hunting day, and that big snake might already be lying full length on a patch of sand or slab of rock, soaking up enough heat to get it moving.

It would be cool underground, and the snake would feel the heat from above. They can come to heat like a coiled spring to a magnet. They are sensitive to even a one-degree change in temperature. When the air cooled at night, they went to ground, because the ground retained the heat. Then by morning when the ground had cooled, the sun was warming the air, so they hurried to come to its light.

Once I thought I had something when I poked into the open end of a long, hollow log, because I felt movement. I probed again, but gently, hoping to startle whatever it was into coming out. When it didn't, I upended the long log and bounced it—and a grizzled, gray possum rolled out.

I walked over and nudged the possum with the toe of my boot, and it lay over on its side and drew its lips back so its teeth showed like they do on dead things. It was a good act, though Dad had once told me that it wasn't an act, that the possum was actually so scared it went into shock and couldn't help itself. He said that's why the possum had survived millions of years without changing while other animals had changed or become extinct.

If it had been closer to evening, I'd have killed the possum to take on back to the shack. But I didn't want to be burdened the rest of the day with a dead possum that by noon would be attracting enough flies to carry it off.

So I nudged it once more to see if it would show some sign of life and then turned away to get on with my snake hunting. When I reached the top of the river bank I looked back, and the possum was scrambling off into the brush.

Once or twice when I came to sandy places that had been washed by high water of the recent heavy rain, I saw snake trails, but I didn't know if they were rattlers or water snakes, except that certainly they hadn't been made by the big one.

At one point along the bank there were panther tracks. I studied them and decided it was a pretty good-sized cat. I knew the Florida panther, which is really a puma, was a lot smaller than its western cousin. But they were big enough to handle a man who was without a weapon (it was against the law to kill them), and anyway what would I do with a panther?

I was snake hunting, and I couldn't afford to let every animal and bird, every track or disturbance on the water, keep distracting me from what I was supposed to do.

So I kept telling myself the day would come, that day when I could wander all day along the river bank or through Big Swampy with nothing to do but to look and listen.

I was covering strips of ground not wider than six feet. Sometimes I could move swiftly because it was obvious there was no place for a snake to hide. But in brushy places I often had to get to my knees and move slowly to investigate every tangle.

I hoped I wouldn't find that snake while crawling on all fours. I might be put somewhat off balance if suddenly right out there in front of my nose the big one was coiled to strike and I was looking right into its slanting slits of eyes.

But it could happen, so I was ready for it. I kept the snake stick out ahead and poked into every place I couldn't see before crawling in and through.

Once or twice while I was hunting I thought I heard pigs squealing. Pigs liked it along the river, because there was always food. They'd eat dead fish, almost anything the river tossed up on its banks.

I had covered about one hundred and fifty rods when the river bank started to slope and dwindle toward lowlands—a bay or inlet. I could hear the pigs plainly now, and knew they were somewhere on the low ground. They sounded excited about something, squealing as their farmyard cousins might when someone was bringing the slop.

Where the ground softened and became squishy there was a fringe of heavy cover. I had to get to my knees to get through, and then as I crawled out again into the open, suddenly there the pigs were.

They were eight of about fifty pounds apiece, standing in a circle around a bog. They were in nearly a foot of water and looked silly because they looked like pigs without legs, like pigs moving around in the muck on their little round bellies.

There was something on the bog they wanted, but they apparently were afraid to attack.

Even little pigs can be vicious. They will attack just about anything they can kill, and they will eat just about anything. Even the barnyard variety will corner chickens or ducks and they'll kill rats and I suppose a dog if they had the chance.

Most people don't know that pigs are such meat eaters. But more than one farmer has made the mistake of falling down inside a pigsty and having a pig start chewing on his leg.

Perhaps the pigs had surrounded a young coon, or maybe even a young bobcat. I entered the water and, leaning on my snake stick, bent forward to see more clearly. What I saw caught me in the throat like somebody had put fingers there.

They had the big snake in the center of their circle and were getting up enough nerve to rush in and trample it to death.

Pigs like snake meat. Probably they like it better than most kinds. If a rancher is running pigs, he usually doesn't have snakes around. I know quail hunters like to hunt on ranches where farmers run pigs. They know their dogs won't be getting hit by snakes.

The snake was coiled and its head, wedge-shaped and large as a flatiron, was poised to hit the first pig that dared come within striking range. Its tongue kept flicking left to right, tasting the pigs, and its stubby, worn rattlers made a grinding little roar as the tail spun back and forth.

If the pigs attacked, one or maybe more would die. But the others would live and they'd eat snake meat.

I'm sure if the pigs had had better footing they would have charged without hesitation. But standing belly-deep in water, they were not sure of themselves. If they rushed the snake, they would meet it on soggy ground into which their sharp little hoofs would sink deeply. They weren't happy about the situation, but they didn't want to give up.

If those pigs killed that snake, if a litter of muddy, grunting, greedy animals snatched my prize right from under my nose. . . .

I got weak thinking about it. I'd been so certain that things were going to work out that in my mind it was already an accomplished fact. My spirits had been so high that it seemed nothing could happen to bring them down. I was confident, so confident I had been making plans way beyond tomorrow, and now a herd of little pigs stood in the way.

I shouted, hoping to scare them off, but they only shifted about and squealed louder. Then a braver one of the eight made as though to attack. Its movements were so clumsy in the water that it just barely missed getting hit when the big snake struck.

Pigs are handy on their feet. They may look clumsy, but they can prance around just out of a snake's thrust range and, when the rattler strikes, dart back; before the snake has a chance to recover, the pigs go in for the kill and trample it to death.

I recovered my wits when I saw that shouting wasn't going to drive the pigs away and started forward to drive them off with my snake stick. The big rattler had obviously been in the water, and its hide, usually the color of the dust it crawled around in, was smooth and gleaming. Shadow and sunlight touched it in different places and, when it moved its head to and fro to keep a count on the pigs, the diamonds on its side and back changed color like autumn leaves twisting and turning in a breeze.

I was running now with water and mud flying. My shouting and splashing distracted the pigs, but they did not retreat. Instead they turned to see if they could handle me.

But I had no fear of a herd of fifty-pound pigs, and could have kicked them out of the way one at a time, if necessary. I'd have routed them, and if I got chewed a little in the bargain, it wouldn't be much of a price to pay.

Once I got rid of the pigs, I could turn my attention to the snake, and I was already planning that attack when a big sow, obviously the mother of the litter, burst into the open and stopped me dead in my tracks.

She was a monster of a pig, and mad. Even though she was not equipped with a boar's tushes, she dug her snout into the water and threw up mud. If only I'd brought the rifle, I could have dropped her in her tracks. But how could I ever have imagined such a crisis to my snake hunt as this?

With the sow standing me off, the little pigs turned their attention back to the snake. Whatever kept me from tackling that sow with my bare hands, I don't know. I wanted that snake so badly there wasn't anything I wouldn't do to get it.

But I collected my wits and put down the rage and the desire to collide with the sow. Instead I backed off slowly so as not to irritate the pig into an attack. And I backed off sick at heart and with a sinking feeling in my stomach. There! There was *my* snake less than five good jumps away and I was helpless to do anything about it.

The sow stood its ground watching my every move. Its unpredictable temper seemed to cool somewhat when it was obvious that I was retreating.

I knew what would happen the instant I got to that

point in my retreat where I was no longer considered a threat or an obstacle. Then the sow would turn her attention to the snake, and the other pigs, encouraged by the reinforcement, would swarm over the snake and in seconds it would be cut to pieces by their sharp hoofs and chomping teeth.

That would be the end of everything. I couldn't take another beating like that. I'd have to tuck my tail between my legs and go crawling like a whipped dog into Evenset and tell Doc and ask for help.

I stopped retreating, hoping the sow's attention would remain focused on me. By not moving back beyond that point where I was no longer a threat, perhaps I could stall the pig's attack on the snake.

All animals have what is known as a critical point of approach. A lion will let a man get just so close, and then spring. Even a dog will ignore another dog if it stays beyond a certain invisible line. And so I knew that if I could find the exact distance at which the pig would not attack yet be held in readiness, I might hold her.

When her interest in me waned, I took a step forward. When she acted angry, I took a step backward. I was wondering how long I could keep it up before the pig would go to the snake or come to me when I glimpsed something swimming in the river. I dared, then, to take my eyes off the sow to see what it was.

Swimming swiftly was an alligator. The commotion in the little bay must have attracted its attention, and now it had the scent of pig in its nostrils and was driving forward with hardly a ripple.

It was a big gator, ten feet if it was an inch. It was brown as the water and swam low until it hit the shallows. Then it lifted a little and I saw the crosshatching on its back.

Ironhead!

I couldn't be mistaken. No two alligators in the world could be marked so exactly alike.

Old Ironhead!

If all the wind hadn't been taken out of my sails by the sudden charge of the big sow, the abrupt and surprising appearance of Ironhead did it.

The little pigs had no idea the alligator was stalking them. They had their attention riveted on the snake. They wanted that snake fast, before I could drive them away from it.

I moved forward a few steps. The sow grunted, put her snout into the water and threw up mud and gnashed her teeth. I backed a few steps to quiet her. Then when her attention strayed, I moved forward again. The sow grunted, but didn't otherwise act angry.

Maybe she was tiring of the game. Perhaps she was coming to realize that I wouldn't attack, and if she wanted that snake all she had to do was walk over and take it.

Now the smaller pigs were getting anxious. They pranced and shouldered one another as they prepared for an attack. I wanted to shout out to distract them, but I was afraid I'd turn Ironhead, send him back into the river.

I took my eyes off the pigs to look at the gator. He

was closing in. Like a great swimming log he was coming through the shallow, muddy waters of the bay, never making a sound.

For a second I forgot about the sow. I couldn't take my eyes off the gator. To myself I said, "Get 'em, Ironhead. Swim fast. Get 'em!"

And I thought I'd seen the last of Ironhead, and here he was. It was like a tableau. All at once all the characters were on the stage. The pigs, Ironhead, the big snake, me. . . .

There was a sudden sound of water, and I turned quickly toward the sow. She was threatening again. It didn't seem as though she'd stand any more. I backed a few steps. She moved forward a few steps.

Then there was a shrill, piercing scream that was almost human. I turned. Ironhead had one of the little pigs by a hind leg. He was turning and twisting and heading for deep water. The other pigs scattered like leaves in front of a wind. Water flew in all directions.

The sow swung away from me to face the new threat. The pig Ironhead had between his jaws squealed again with terror. It was too much for the sow. She backed a few steps, whirled, and disappeared into the scrub.

It didn't take Ironhead long after that. He hit the deep water, the pig squealed once more and then gurgled as they disappeared. The water bulged and boiled as Ironhead twisted and turned his victim to tear it apart so he could eat it.

Everything had happened so swiftly, my mind

hadn't kept up with it. I had been watching Ironhead and forgotten about the snake, and when I turned it was gone from the bog.

I ran forward, but there was no sign of it. Assuming the snake had headed for high ground, I splashed through the bay toward the nearest bank and when I came out of the water I saw the snake's trail in the mud.

I hurried up the side of the bank and, coming over the top to the sunny side, almost ran the snake over. It was moving like writhing lightning, and even as I ran I aimed my forked stick and brought it down behind the neck, which was as thick around as the calf of my leg.

I squeezed as hard as I dared. I had to keep the snake pinned to the ground, but I couldn't risk injuring it. It threshed and I had to jump to avoid being hit.

I had pinned down hundreds of snakes before, but never anything like this. It seemed to have the power of ten snakes, and the stick throbbed in my hands.

It would surely kill itself. Sticks and small stones and dirt went flying. It coiled and straightened and writhed from side to side. I had to bag it at once, there was never any doubt in my mind about that.

I went to one knee, and then, instead of using a thumb and forefinger as I did with other snakes, I took a full handgrip on the snake just in back of the head.

Dropping the stick I stood up. The snake whipped about in my grasp like it was loaded with electricity. Even when I was on my feet, more than half the snake was still on the ground.

I swung the sack around just as the snake convulsed into a loop. I slid the loop into the sack. Gradually I increased the pressure of my grip and the snake began relaxing. Then I folded it over onto itself until the rattles and the head were at eye level. I loosened my hold and the big snake dropped into the sack.

I closed the mouth of the sack and, holding it with both hands, walked back into the shade. The sack vibrated for a few seconds, and then except for some undulating movements as the snake sought to discover where it was, the rattler was still. I tied the sack, and cutting some palmetto, covered the sack so the darkness would be complete. The snake made no movement. I could hear nothing.

I had done it. I had the snake. I had won. This was the beginning of the end of our lives in Big Swampy. I should have been overjoyed. Perhaps I should have run up and down the river bank laughing and shouting and singing. There should have been such a good feeling inside as I'd never felt.

But I was only tired. I was so tired I had to lie down. I felt like I had walked a hundred miles under a blazing sun and finally reached the shade. My mind felt like a squeezed sponge with all the wonderful thoughts drained out of it. It felt empty as an opened coconut.

Maybe I had dreamed too much, tried too hard. I walked to the river bank and slipped out of my clothes. Looking around to make sure there were no snakes or alligators, I slid off into the cool, brown water. It pressed around me and I dove under. I swam, holding my breath until I thought my lungs must burst. Then

I surfaced and gasped for air. Swimming slowly then, I came to shore.

I lay half in and half out of the water looking up through the cypress trees. A tree duck drake, brilliant as a washed rainbow, flew past. In a few seconds the drab hen came by, cocking her head from left to right to see what inlet or bay her husband had popped into.

A frog across the river jumped from a hyacinth pad and missed the one it was aiming for. There was a swirl and water flew as a trout ended life for that frog.

Maybe I was wrong, but it seemed my mind could handle just so much and then it got behind. And when it got behind, I got to feeling low.

But it was catching up now. I could feel it, because I was beginning to notice things. Like the Mexican eagle high above and soaring for a little while, then slanting down and down and out of sight probably to get its talons into a snake. They are great snake killers.

Finally I felt like getting up. I shook myself and sent water flying. Then I dressed and went back and uncovered the snake. I lifted the sack. It was heavy. It would be hard to carry without continually bumping it with a leg. I tied it to the end of the snake stick, put it over my shoulder, and started toward the shack.

With every step my spirits rose again. I began to feel better as the full meaning of my accomplishment worked around in my mind.

I had finally caught the snake. I had it here in a sack. I was taking it to the shack. And tomorrow Dad and I would walk down to the road. Tomorrow we'd start down another road, the road back.

CHAPTER 12

꙰ That night I could savor my victory. I sat for a long time on the log beside Dad and watched the stars. The real feeling of having come to the end of a long, hard journey was in me. I tried to tell Dad about it. About how I had caught the big snake, and right now that snake was in the dark, cool hole where I kept snakes awaiting delivery to Diamond Springs. I told him we were going to go to the city where he'd get help, and then one day when he was better we'd come back.

The next morning I began to collect the few things I wanted to take along. I had decided not to take much. I'd leave most of everything except the clothes we needed. Then if we wanted to or got the chance, some-day maybe we could come back for weekends or vacations.

When we had left our home in Evenset, I had

thought it was going to be a vacation. It had seemed we'd only catch enough snakes and hunt and fish enough to keep us in food, and then be lazy the rest of every day.

But then I had anticipated that a week in Big Swampy was going to be all Dad needed to get him on his feet. I had believed that he would be roaming the country with me, helping catch possum and coon and fish and snakes, and walking to Evenset for groceries and back again in the cool of the evening.

I had anticipated that we would enjoy the days and especially the evenings, grunting up Ironhead and going to the watering holes to watch the deer come down.

But, of course, it hadn't worked that way. Dad had gotten worse from the very moment we stepped down off the white porch in Evenset. And, instead of having a holiday, I'd had my hands full taking care of Dad and trying to get enough food on the table to keep us alive.

Well, it was over now, and it seemed the days we had lived in Evenset were a thousand years in the past, and sometimes they didn't even seem real any more, and I'd catch myself wondering if I hadn't dreamed it all.

When I looked back across the nearly two months since we'd come down the street with our packs, I saw a little boy following his father away from the village out into the scrub. Then it was I had to get out front and do the leading, and now, if I wasn't a man, I was a pretty good imitation of one.

I'd have to take the rifle too, because I was afraid someone might break in and steal it. It was too good a gun to leave behind. But the bedding, dishes, extra clothes, the few books, the jack light, what food was left . . . most things would be left behind.

While I was securing the pack, my eyes kept turning to where Dad was sitting on the log hunched into himself. I wondered if the doctors would find some way to jolt him out of himself into the clear, to come alive again. Or would he just drift off his days hardly knowing what he was eating and caring less? Whatever happened, at least now I'd be better able to care for him.

Whatever *did* happen, I don't think I could ever forget what an all-alive person Dad had once been. It seemed to me that a man who had everything going for him like that just couldn't stay in some half-world of dimness and memories.

Someday something would have to crack that wall he'd built around his mind, and when that day came . . . *when* . . . *when* that day came. . . .

I laced the canvas tight and carried the gun and the pack outside and sat it near the end of the log. Then I went back in to finish up. I poured flour, sugar, and salt from their bags into cans so the mice wouldn't get into it, and it would be nice to have when we came back. I poured what grits and rice was left into cans, just in case we got a chance to use it.

There was some meat left, but I threw it out for the birds. I got the butter dish up from the hole and cleaned it. There were a dozen cans of beans and I stacked them on a shelf alongside of a few cans of peaches.

When everything was in order, I swept the shack

out, and then put everything up in the rafters—bedding and all—where the mice weren't so likely to get into it. Then I looked around to see if I'd forgotten anything.

I had a feeling of homesickness. It was going to be hard leaving the shack, even though I hadn't really been happy there. But I'd had experiences I'd never forget. And, there'd been nice days too, when everything went off on schedule and I came tired to my bed and could lie there and watch moonlight creep across the floor.

If I'd learned anything, it was to hang on no matter how tough the day because tomorrow might be better —even wonderful.

Little things, I learned, were especially nice—like cool rain after a siege of hot weather. A nice breeze at night or a potful of possum and some fluffy rice. Iron-head grunting. Birds circling. Hooty owls talking it up. Spider webs with morning mist caught in bright drops.

Anyway, right now I was just about ready to burst right through my shirt. When I walked into Diamond Springs with that big snake, wouldn't their eyes pop? Mr. Shen would call the newspaper people and they'd send a reporter and photographer. Everybody in the office would quit work and crowd around to see the snake and to ask me how I'd caught it.

Then after the snake had been put into a pit, I'd walk into Mr. Shen's office and he'd make me tell the story of catching it all over again, and the reporter would be listening and taking notes. Then he'd hand me the check for five-hundred dollars, and I know he'd say: "First time in thirty years. I swear I never thought I'd have to pay it, because I never believed there was a rattler that big."

Then he'd probably joke and say: "Doug, you sure you weren't stuffing possums down that critter to make it grow? How long you had it in captivity? Did you start it from a little snake, or did you start off and feed a six-footer until it grew to eight feet?"

Then everybody would laugh, and I'd joke back and say I got it when it was a foot long and force-fed it five times a day with chicken eggs.

Pretty soon then, Doc Bellamy would come driving over, and we'd sit and have a talk about Dad.

But I couldn't keep my mind on the dark side of things. The day was too beautiful and the snake was too big and we were going out!

I went out the door of the shack for the last time, and making sure I had the key in my pocket, slapped the lock in place and snapped it shut.

Then I went over to the log where Dad was sitting and knelt to hoist the pack to my shoulders. Then I'd pick up the snake and we could be on our way. I had both hands on the straps and had just begun to lift when I raised my eyes and there, not two feet from me, was the head of that big snake.

I froze. Every muscle went rigid. I made my eyes not blink. One move and the snake would hit, and he'd get me in the face. A silly picture of me with a tourniquet around my neck flashed across my mind. Only it wasn't funny. That snake's long fangs were loaded with enough poison to lay low a cow.

The snake's rattles whirred and the sound was like a piece of sandpaper being rubbed across my brain. I glanced from the corner of my eye at where Dad was sitting on the log hoping he wouldn't move and provoke the snake into striking. Dad had turned and was facing, and looking directly at both of us.

"My God! My God!" I kept saying it over and over in my mind. It was all I could think of. My mind seemed almost paralyzed at the closeness of the snake.

I had always thought snakes looked beautiful, but now the flat, diamond-shaped head with its cold, calculating eyes looked evil. The snake was coiled layer on layer until its head and the flicking tongue were nearly two feet off the ground. It probably could strike with the force of a thrown stone, and the long, curved fangs might get so hooked into my face that the snake could not retract them.

I didn't dare breathe. I knew that even a falling leaf might irritate it into striking. Anything, a stem of grass moving in the breeze, a butterfly alighting on the log. . . .

Above all I didn't dare blink. If my eyes moved the snake's head would surely flash out. Tears started to accumulate and I felt them standing in my eyes.

How *had* that snake escaped? I was sure the string was tight. It could only have been the warmth of the sun. Sensitive to the comforting temperatures above its damp, dank hole, the snake must have writhed until it wore a hole through the side of the sack or slipped the string.

I should have taken into consideration its extraordinary power. It was so strong I had hardly been able to hold it. And its tough old skin was as abrasive when covered with dust as a grinding stone. Two flimsy grain sacks probably had parted threads, and once there was the tiniest of openings, the snake probably widened it into a hole through which it could squirm.

The snake's head weaved back and forth slowly, and I had no trouble understanding how a bird or small animal might be almost hypnotized. There was something fascinating about the easy, almost sleepy swaying, about the old eyes, the probing tongue, and the monotonous whirr of rattles.

Try as I would, I couldn't make my mind behave. Without meaning to, I felt the urge to move my head in time to the snake's. I could feel my whole body wanting to sway back and forth. The absolute horror of the situation was escaping me, draining away in fascination. The dread that had first seized me had been quieted. I was losing the will to want to escape.

Then I think that perhaps my head did begin to move slowly and rhythmically in time with the snake's. I could feel my eyes roll from side to side. Everything around me ceased to exist, and the center of everything, the whole world, was right there in the snake's eyes.

I don't know if I was hypnotized or if the complete hopelessness of my predicament had put a merciful blanket over my mind. At times I'd feel my mind groping toward reality and for a second or two fear would return. At times I'd get a hold of myself long enough to know that if the snake hit me I might die.

But always my mind would slip slowly and softly back and down, lower and lower and farther and farther away until it seemed all wrapped up and warm in cotton—comfortable, content.

"Duck, Doug!"

The words blasted through the cotton around my mind like bullets to a target. I ducked, and the snake's head was out of my line of visibility.

"Roll, Doug!"

And I rolled over and over, and then I looked back to see Dad standing over the snake, beating it with the snake stick that I had left leaning against the log.

I lay for a few seconds to give my mind time to accept what my eyes were seeing. Then I was on my feet and running. When I got to the log, the snake was dead.

I looked up from the still twitching body into Dad's face. There was a bright look of recognition in his eyes. His lips had turned up at the corners in the start of a smile.

Then he came over and threw his arms around me.

"Doug, Doug, I've never been so scared," he said. "Never, never in my whole life."

I felt strength in his arms. I felt his tears on the back of my neck. I heard a small sob deep down in his chest —the first since Mother had died.

CHAPTER 13

We took the snake's body with us. I put the pack on my back and wrapped the dead snake around my neck. We went down the trail, but this time I wasn't leading. Dad was out front. He didn't hurry. He walked slowly and carefully like he was learning. But the shuffle was gone out of his step.

Sometimes he'd stop to rest. Then he'd turn, and there must have been such amazement in my face he had to say: "It's all right, Doug. It's really all right."

And it must have been close to noon when we came near enough to hear the hum of tires on the highway. Then before we broke out of the scrub I heard voices.

There down the trail came Doc Bellamy, Mr. Shen, and Mr. Bowles. "We were just coming in for a visit," Doc said, shaking Dad's hand. "Say," he looked Dad up and down, "but you've lost a lot of weight. Been eating your own cooking?"

Mr. Shen was examining the snake. "I'd never have believed it," he was saying over and over. "I'll give you two hundred and fifty dollars to mount it for my museum."

I couldn't say anything. Doc was making introductions. They were all examining the snake. I didn't want to say anything. It was nice not to have to say anything—just to be a boy in the background.

"Can we give you a ride?" Mr. Shen was asking Dad.

"We'd be much obliged," Dad said.

Then we walked and I fell a little way behind. Mr. Shen was asking Dad if he had any job in mind, or if he was going back to his old one, but maybe would he consider working at the Reptile Institute?

I didn't hear Dad's answer, because I had stopped and was looking back over a waving sea of yellow saw grass to where the green cabbage hammocks began. And darn it all, there were tears in my eyes again.

Born and brought up in central Wisconsin, outdoorsman Mel Ellis fished, hunted, and trapped at an early age. By the time he went into journalism after graduating from the University of Notre Dame, he was an ardent conservationist and conceived, wrote, and edited what was probably the first complete page of conservation news ever carried by a newspaper. In 1961, he was named Wisconsin Conservation Writer of the Year. Not surprisingly, conservation sounds an important note in his books, *Sad Song of the Coyote*, *Ironhead*, *Run, Rainy, Run* and *Softly Roars the Lion*. In 1968, he was awarded the Council for Wisconsin Writers' highest award when *Run, Rainy, Run* was named the outstanding literary work of the preceding year.

Mr. Ellis has seen both ends of the world of journalism: as outdoor editor of the *Milwaukee Journal* and associate editor of *Field and Stream;* and as author of several hundred articles and stories in magazines as widely disassociated as *National Geographic* and *True, The Man's Magazine*.

Mel Ellis has "fished and hunted the continent from end to end,"—including the Florida Everglades, setting of *Ironhead*—but his favorite spot is his fifteen acre Wisconsin spread of trout and warm water fish ponds. Appropriately called Little Lakes, it also has almost every tree native to Wisconsin and was put together "with *sweat,* blood and tears." He lives here with his wife and five daughters.